Uncle Rudolf

Uncle Rudolf

Paul Bailey

ST. MARTIN'S PRESS ★ NEW YORK

www.stmartins.com

Library of Congress Cataloging-in-Publication Data

Bailey, Paul, 1937–
    Uncle Rudolf / Paul Bailey.—1st U.S. ed.
        p. cm.
    ISBN 0-312-31834-0
    1. Romanians—Foreign countries—Fiction. 2. Reminiscing in old age—Fiction. 3. Failure (Psychology)—Fiction. 4. Refugees—Fiction. 5. Aged men—Fiction. 6. Singers—Fiction. 7. Uncles—Fiction. 8. Europe—Fiction. I. Title.

PR6052.A319U53 2004
813'.54—dc22   2003058773

First published in Great Britain by Fourth Estate, a division of HarperCollinsPublishers

First U.S. Edition: February 2004

10 9 8 7 6 5 4 3 2 1

For Norman and Cella Manea

'A wand'ring minstrel I,
A thing of shreds and patches . . .'

Sung by Nanki-Poo in *The Mikado*.
Words by W.S. Gilbert

'I hate operetta'

György Ligeti, in a radio interview

I woke up yesterday morning with the old words on my tongue. There they were again, for the third time this year. In those first moments of consciousness, I could hear myself talking of blood and snow and storks on chimney tops in the language I put behind me. The disconnected phrases made no sense at all, but I understood their meaning.

— Shut up, I said aloud, in English. Go back where you belong.

Where do they belong? In my earliest childhood, I suppose, when I had a mother and a father. I spoke them as a little boy, whose name was Andrei, in the country I left at the age of seven. I babbled them, rather, the way children babble. Yes, I have a memory of babbling about the snow as it fell and then settled, turning – I imagined – the whole world white.

— There is no snow in India and Africa, my father corrected me. Except high up on the mountains. The Indians and Africans who live on the ground never see it.

I was sorry for the Indians and Africans who lived on the ground, because I loved to watch the snowflakes falling from heaven, making that beautiful carpet.

The young dentist who examined me this afternoon commented on the remarkable condition of my teeth. He was surprised that a man of seventy should have a mouth so free from decay. My gums had receded, of course, which was only natural, and there was a small amount of plaque, but otherwise, dentally speaking, I was in splendid shape. He showed me my healthy molars on a closed circuit television screen as proof.

— You have taken good care of yourself, Mr Peters.

I did not tell him, or his wife, the hygienist who disposed of the plaque, that I had to thank Uncle Rudolf for my strong teeth. The story would have struck them as absurd. It is true, even so.

— Andrew, said my uncle (Andrei had become

Andrew on the platform at Victoria Station, on the evening of the twenty-third of February 1937, minutes after my arrival.) Andrew, he said to me over breakfast the next day, that is burnt toast you are staring at. Cover it with jam by all means, or spread some butter on it, but eat it, if you please. I want to hear you crunching on it.

— Yes, Uncle, I responded dutifully, although I was mystified. My father had advised me to obey Uncle Rudolf's every command.

I crunched on the blackened toast.

— Bravo, Andrew. Keep crunching.

I wondered if, perhaps, he was mad. I was only seven years old, but I knew something about madness already. There was a man who often stood outside the courthouse where my father worked as the chief clerk shouting that there was no justice but God's. Human justice was a mirage, a phantom, he proclaimed. This man, who had a beard that went down to his knees – 'To conceal eternal shame' – was regarded as a harmless lunatic. He had nothing dangerous in his nature, my father reassured me. I was to pity him. I was to pity all those like him.

Would I have to pity Uncle Rudolf? He was smiling at me as I kept on crunching, and his

3

smile was not that of a madman, I decided. No, he was not one of the unhappy souls my father had alerted me to.

— I was introduced to burnt toast, Andrew, by a Negro with a gleaming smile in a funny place called Hollywood. I expressed admiration for the dazzling whiteness of his teeth, and he told me his secret was burnt toast. He had been eating it all his life, like his parents before him.

Where was this funny place? I asked my uncle.

— You must be the one boy on the planet not to know where Hollywood is. It is in America, Andrew. In California, to be exact. It is the home of Mickey Mouse and Donald Duck. It is where motion pictures are made. I was there a couple of years ago, playing – and singing – the part of Barinkay in *The Gypsy Baron*. The movie was never completed. I was paid my wages and I came home to Europe, a sadder and a richer man. You are looking bewildered and your tea is getting cold.

I was aware that Uncle Rudolf was a famous singer – the whole town knew of his fame – but this talk of Hollywood was beyond my understanding.

— Have you never seen a motion picture, Andrew?

— No, I confessed. Mamă says I must be protected from the cinema until I am older.

— Does she? She is strict in her faith, if I remember.

— Yes, Uncle.

— I will take you to the pictures today, if you eat up your toast and drink your tea. You deserve a treat after your long journey.

I crunched with a purpose and drained my cup.

— Where is she, Uncle? Can you tell me?

— No, to be honest. I wish I could. Your mother is safe somewhere, that much I can tell you.

Safe. Somewhere. On Uncle Rudolf's lips, the words were comforting. The old words, of course.

Am I attempting to stave off the prospect of my second childhood? Why else, I ask myself, should I now be writing about my life with Rudolf Peterson, who was born Rudi Petrescu? Walking the five miles back from the dentist's today, at my usual brisk pace, in light rain, I realized that I had said goodbye to his receptionist in Romanian. *La revedere*: these were my last words to my father, spoken with a sob as the train drew out of the Gare du Nord in Paris, on the morning of the twenty-third of February, 1937. I went on waving to him until he and I were out of each other's sight. Although I was sad to be parted from him, I was also happily innocent of his impending plan to disappear.

— Your uncle will take care of you, Andrei. For the time being – weeks, maybe months. No longer, dear one, I promise. This will be a holiday for you. Rudi is an amusing man. He will make you laugh. He has stories at his fingertips.

My father entrusted me to the care of a guard, with whom he communicated in French and a few, telling signs. The man nodded his understanding of the task ahead of him, muttering *Oui, Monsieur* and *Je comprends* and, finally, *Merci beaucoup, Monsieur* when he accepted the francs my father offered him. He was to deliver me, *petit* Andrei – Andrei, Andrei, my father repeated – into the hands of Maestro Rudolf Peterson, who would be waiting for his nephew on the station platform in London. Then my father produced from the inside pocket of his best overcoat a photograph of my uncle dressed, I think, as a pirate, with a bandanna on his head, large rings in his ears and a cutlass in his belt. My father entreated the guard to study the maestro's face, and nothing else. The man did so, and smiled. The maestro, my father insisted, would be wearing ordinary clothes.

Not *très ordinaire*, but *ordinaire*. No earrings; no sword. The man nodded vigorously, still smiling.

— *La revedere*, Tată, I managed to say, although I was choking with fear and anticipation. I did not want this holiday. I wanted to be with my mother and father, from whom I had never been separated. Yet I also wanted to meet my famous Uncle Rudolf – to listen to the stories he had at his fingertips; to have him sing for me.

I have Jewish blood in my veins, but I can't ascertain how much. Does it constitute a third, a quarter, a half of me? A sixteenth, perhaps, or less? Will it ever be possible to quantify a person's blood – to say, with conviction, that those drops are Norse, those Gallic, those Latin, those Tatar? Mine has yet to be quantified, but what is certain is that some of it is Jewish.

My mother's father was a Jew. He was known in the town, even after his death – which happened before I was born – as the Debt Collector. My maternal grandmother enraged and upset her parents when she declared her love for him. She was stubborn, and had her way, against all their modest hopes and wishes for her. She stated, quite calmly, that she

would end her life if she could not marry him. And
he, in turn, angered his own family by saying that no
other girl but Doina would ever make him happy.

They were married in a nearby city, to escape the
gossip in the town. It was said that he renounced
his faith, but he had no faith to renounce. He was
a freethinker, an atheist, and might have been a
professor or a scholar if his father had not died
suddenly. He became a reluctant middleman instead,
collecting money from the peasants who lived and
toiled on the Haşdeu estate. It was necessary for him
to earn a living, and – like a fool, he said afterwards
– he allowed himself to continue the family tradition.
The eldest son – and he was an only child – was
expected to be the next intermediary, doing the
landowner's nasty work for him. And that is what
my grandfather did, with much sorrow and anguish,
my mother told me.

He was already dead when, in 1935, the saviour of
the Romanian people, the Pied Piper who would lead
them to a Balkan paradise, stood on the steps of the
courthouse and exhorted his disciples to free themselves from the Jewish yoke. My mother and father
were among the crowd who listened to Corneliu
Zelea Codreanu as he recounted how he had stood

before an icon of the Archangel Michael in the chapel of the prison at Vacareşti and received immediate and lasting inspiration. The tall, dark Codreanu had the blazing eyes, the trumpet-like voice of a prophet, my father revealed to me later. His kind of prophet was best left in the wilderness, talking to stones and trees and passing birds, but alas Codreanu was not in the wilderness, my father complained. He was here, there and everywhere, in the very heart of the country.

Thinking of the Pied Piper and what he represented, I am driven to set down a scene from childhood – my only childhood, I hope. It is a Thursday morning in early September. The year is 1936. I am with my mother at the market in the town square. The weather has turned chilly. She has a scarf on her head and a shawl about her shoulders, and I am sweltering inside the lamb's wool jacket she has forced me to wear. She is bartering with the stallholder who sells cabbages, as is the custom. She wants the firmest, greenest cabbage he has, at a price she can afford. Cabbage soup is her husband's favourite dish, she tells the stallholder, who remarks that without cabbage soup he would have no business. My mother brings out her purse; she haggles a little more; the stallholder observes, as he observes to all the women on every market day, that she will make a pauper of him, and then her lip is trembling, and her hands are shaking, and I am suddenly afraid for her. She has just heard a woman behind her say:

— That's the Debt Collector's daughter, damn her, striking a hard bargain.

My mother gives the stallholder the coins and rushes off. I pick up the purse she has dropped, and take the cabbage she has bought, and look at the woman who caused my mother to shake and tremble and run away. She is fat and red-faced and she is gloating – yes, that is the word I can use of her now, but did not know then – she is gloating with pride at the harm she has done. I stare at her. Do I want her to call me the Debt Collector's grandson? I wait. I want her to give me a reason to spit at her. Her gaze shifts to the stallholder, and I hear her telling him his cabbages are too costly, in almost the same words my mother had spoken a minute earlier.

My mother was devoutly Orthodox. My father would joke that there weren't enough saints' days in the year to satisfy her. On the day of the cabbage she came home and prayed to the icon of the Virgin and Child for what seemed hours. I heard her implore the

Holy Mother to forgive the woman who had insulted
her and her dear father's memory, and to cleanse the
minds and hearts of all those in the town who thought
the same.

Our dinner that evening was, naturally, cabbage
soup, into which my mother stirred a generous dollop
of soured cream, to please my father. I kept my promise and did not mention the woman in the market. We
ate contentedly. Many years later, I saw a picture in
the Rijksmuseum in Amsterdam, by one of the minor
Dutch masters, that might have captured the three of
us – a happy trinity – at table. There was the tureen;
there were the bowls, and there were the father, the
mother and the greedy little boy, whose own empty
bowl would soon, he hoped, be filled again. They
were bathed in a light that reflected their beatific
state, while the room behind them was in darkness.
A warm darkness, I thought, into which you could
steal with safety.

— What is so special about Mr De Witt's picture,
Andrew? There are hundreds like it here.

— It appeals to me, Uncle. It speaks to me, as you
say. I find it rather moving.

— If you find that moving, you will be overwhelmed
by the Rembrandts, should we ever get to them,

you young slowcoach. I can confidently predict that your emotional floodgates will open and burst. Leave those humble folk to their soup, Andrew. Come along.

I could not tell him that the picture had sent me drifting back to the peaceful evening of the cabbage soup and the terrible day of the cabbage which preceded it. That's the Debt Collector's daughter, damn her, striking a hard bargain – the woman's voice was in my head as I walked beside Uncle Rudolf, who was impatient to show me real masterpieces. Those persons for ever unknown made off with the Debt Collector's daughter, not my devout and innocent mother.

I squeezed my protector's arm, very gently, when we came to a stop in front of *The Night Watch*, in unsaid gratitude for his protection.

The sky was black when we set off on our long journey. The snow was so hard that it didn't crackle under our feet. My father lifted me on to Mircea the woodman's cart and then jumped up and lay beside me. He covered us, quickly, with a rough blanket.

— Lie still, Andrei, he whispered. Lie very still.

— I want to sneeze. There's dust in my nose.

— And in mine.

— Are we hiding from people, Tată?

— Bogies. Lots of them. We must be silent, Andrei dear.

I was proud of myself for not having sneezed when my father lowered me to the ground. I looked about me for bogies, but there were none to be seen. Mircea's old horse neighed loudly, and I told him to be quiet, whereupon he opened his huge mouth, which was yellow inside, and yawned. I noticed in amazement that the woodman was crying.

— Wickedness, said Mircea. Wickedness. Wickedness.

— My good friend. You are my good friend.

— Wickedness. Mircea wiped away the tears from his cheeks with the back of his gloved hand. Wickedness.

— Say goodbye and thank you to Mircea, Andrei.

But before I could speak, the grizzled woodman (it occurs to me now that Mircea's face was definitely grizzled) was pressing me to him with such force that I found it hard to breathe. He bent down and kissed me and I felt his grey stubble pricking my skin.

— The train will soon be here, said my father. He

took some notes from his pocket, but Mircea refused them with an offended snort. Do not wait with us, my friend. Return to your bed.

Mircea was reluctant to leave us, I remember. It was only the horse's restlessness – he was neighing again, and stamping his hooves – that persuaded him to go. There was a final embrace, and then he climbed into the driver's seat. The horse needed no encouragement to move.

We were left alone. We were alone together for an eternity. How often, in reveries and dreams, has our lonely vigil come back to me – the two of us, disheartened father and apprehensive son, cuddling each other closely, for warmth as much as reassurance, on the tiny station's solitary bench, and waiting, waiting.

— We must be careful not to fall asleep, Andrei. The train will only stop if we wave it down.

— Yes, Tată.

— There's been a snowstorm, I expect, further up the line.

It was almost dawn before the train arrived. Its distant chugging awakened startled crows and sparrows. We stood up and shook our limbs. My father put out his arm as the train drew slowly into the tiny station

and then passed through it, only stopping to leave us
a choice between the last three carriages. It was the
middle one we settled for, because it was empty.

— You can sleep now, if you wish, Andrei. You can
spread yourself out and sleep.

— Tell me some more about Uncle Rudolf, Tată.
Will I like him?

— Oh, yes. Have no fear. Unless you are a very
dull and stupid boy, which I know you are not, you
will certainly like him. You could not be going to a
better uncle.

From the window, for mile upon mile, we saw
nothing but snow and dun-coloured sky. We passed
a village, where the peasants' huts had been transformed into igloos.

— Igloos, Tată, I said, pointing at the huts that
no longer seemed to be made of wood. My father
had taught me how Eskimos live, snug inside their
ice-houses. He was pleased that I hadn't forgotten the
lesson. It was his ambition, as a lover of geography, to
travel the world – all of it, hot and cold – and study
the customs of other peoples. In the meantime, he
joked, I have been everywhere in my head, tapping
it to ensure that I understood what he was saying. He
had read about the Eskimos, and the many tribes of

Africa, and the Grand Canyon, and the Sahara Desert in the French edition of *National Geographic*, the magazine he had begun to collect. There were several copies of it on our bookshelf, next to my story books, the Bible, and *Family Medicine*, which my mother consulted when my father or I caught a cold or came down with a fever. *Family Medicine* had a simple cure for every ordinary illness. It was more reliable than the doctor she once called in to look at me, whose hands were shaky from drink.

The train stopped abruptly – at another tiny country station – and a man got into the carriage we had hoped would be ours alone. He had the look of a soldier, in his heavy greatcoat and shiny boots.

— It is bitter out there, he told us, slamming the door behind him and slapping his sides. Where are you heading for?

— The capital, my father answered.

— On business?

— Yes, that is right. On business.

— What business would that be?

— Legal business. I work for lawyers.

— Honest lawyers?

— I have no reason to believe they are dishonest.

— Watch them closely, nevertheless. They are not always to be trusted.

— I thank you for your advice. My father was being (I understand now) sarcastic.

— Is this handsome young fellow yours? The man smiled at me. I think I tried to smile back.

— He is, yes. His name is Andrei.

— He is the image of his father. He has something of your fine nose already. Good day to you, Andrei.

— Good day, sir.

The man gave his name, which was Constantin Florescu. It has lodged in my memory for sixty-three years.

My father introduced himself, accepting a cigarette from the gold case Constantin Florescu opened with a flick.

— And is Andrei destined for the law?

— It is too early to say. He is a bright child. Shut your ears, Andrei, while I pay you compliments. He has curiosity and imagination. Perhaps a little too much imagination.

— That will pass. Childhood is the time to be imaginative. After which, sense prevails. In some cases, he added with a sneer. You will learn, Andrei

17

Petrescu, that some men are more sensible than others. As for women, they are divinely blessed. They have no need of sense. Do not make too much money when you grow up. Women will spend it for you.

— I trust my son will not involve himself with such women. I hope he will find a woman with his mother's character.

— And where is that good lady? At home?

My father hesitated.

— At home. Of course.

— I shall marry one day, Constantin Florescu announced. He stroked his thick moustache. I shall pick my wife with care. If it is God's wish, as it is mine, she will give me sons.

— Ah, yes, said my father. God's wish. Andrei is going to England. For a month or so.

— England? Why not Germany?

— We have a relative in England.

— A Romanian relative?

— Naturally.

— The English are not good to us. The English are playing games with us. They were our allies a few years ago. But now they are suspicious of our plans to build a greater, stronger country, said

Constantin Florescu, undoing the buttons on his overcoat, revealing a green shirt.

— You are a Guardist, my father remarked, calmly.

— Indeed I am.

— So you put your faith in the prophet Codreanu, with his vision of a pure Romania.

— I do. As do all true patriots.

The train was nearing Bucharest. There were no more igloos. I saw tall buildings and tramcars and men and women walking along the pavements. The town of my birth dwindled as I stared out at the bustling city.

We said goodbye to our companion when we reached the ticket barrier.

— I am fighting on your behalf, Andrei Petrescu. Remind your father of that. What a very small suitcase you are taking with you to England.

I am writing in one of the leather-bound ledgers in which – like Teddy Grubb before me – I used to enter my uncle's earnings. I think I am writing to reclaim my own life – my sheltered protected life – as much as his, Uncle Rudolf's, because the compulsion to bring the past into the present will not be stilled. I can barely sleep, so urgent is the task I have set myself. Healthy as I am, ridiculously young as I might appear, I am nevertheless conscious that death could forestall me.

The benevolent Saint Nicholas is above the desk, smiling a just-detectable half-smile. The wonder-worker is blessing me with his right hand.

— If anything bad ever happens to God, we have always got Saint Nicholas. My uncle was fond of the old Russian saying, and often quoted it whenever he stopped to look at his beloved icon.

— Nobody knows who painted him, Andrew. The artist was without worldly ambition. He had his gift and his faith, and the two came together when he picked up his brush. You will care for my precious icon when I am dead, won't you?

— Yes, Uncle, I answered, not wanting to imagine a life beyond his.

— You promise me?

— Yes, Uncle. I promise.

He embraced me then, and ruffled my hair, and said that the impossible country of Moldania beckoned. He would be exiled for three silly hours, during which distracted time he would inspire the peasants to revolt in a friendly manner – No bloodshed, I implore you! – before discovering he was their long-lost king.

— Oh, Andrew, will I never be freed from this nonsense?

Murături was the old word on my lips this morning. Why was I thinking of pickled vegetables – of cauliflower and carrots; of green and red peppers; of radishes and red cabbage? I hadn't eaten the dish in a lifetime, not since . . . and then, with an involuntary cry of anguish, I pictured a lake, and clear blue sky, and saw my mother and me tickling my father, who is pretending to be asleep on the grass. The vegetables are glistening on little plates on that summer afternoon in 1936.

Why has this scene – of the kind so many English poets call sylvan – never come to me in dreams?

— I will have my revenge, you scamp, says my father, waking with a start, as if from a nightmare.

His revenge, his sweet revenge, is to tickle his son's tummy, until the happy boy is weak with giggling.

I did not know you could kill hours until that afternoon in Bucharest.

— We have hours to kill, Andrei. We must think of something to do. Are you hungry?

— A little bit. How do you kill hours, Tată?

— By keeping busy. You kill time by forgetting about it. You pretend it doesn't exist. Let's see if Cina is open.

I have a memory of crossing a huge square in order to reach my uncle's favourite restaurant. I see again a fat, bald waiter greeting my father as we enter Cina, stamping the snow from our boots. The waiter knows my father's brother from the time he broke the hearts of every woman in the city. There was never a Danilo more wickedly handsome.

— How is the great Rudolf?

— He is well, Sandu. This young man is his nephew. Andrei is going to London to live with him for a while.

Sandu brings us the dishes the great Rudolf Peterson most enjoys and we eat as much as we can. My father drinks the red wine his brother loves and soon the hours we needed to kill have gone by, only to recur in vivid snatches, a whole lifetime later, in the dreams that beset an Englishman named Andrew Peters. The beaming Sandu is shaking my hand and saying:

— Tell your uncle, the moment you meet him, that he must come back to his country. Tell him that is

Sandu's command. We do not have many heroes, Andrei, but Rudolf Peterson is one of them. Remind him that he is a national hero.

I promised to pass on the message and did so, on the twenty-third of February, 1937, on the platform at Victoria Station. It was something to say to the man who had lifted me up in his arms till my face was level with his. Uncle Rudolf laughed, and kissed me on both cheeks.

— I am no hero, Andrew. I am a hero on the stage, but nowhere else.

The final part of my last, week-long journey with my father took three days. We crossed the Hungarian plains in darkness, with only the black shapes of trees visible from the window. Then there were the mountains of Austria and Switzerland to marvel at. The French countryside, which I would visit with Uncle Rudolf in the autumn of 1950, when he was intent on educating me in matters of the spirit, seemed dull by contrast.

The train stopped at each border. Soldiers carrying guns came aboard and examined everybody's papers. I remember that one of them, an Austrian or perhaps a German, pulled a frightened face in mockery of my own. His feigned look of terror made me smile, but it angered my father, who muttered words the man understood, for he instantly reassumed his stern expression.

I wasn't scared of the guns, in truth. It was the future, of which I had been unaware before, that caused me to be fearful. I knew this solely from the gnawing pain in my stomach, which spoke of things unknown. A similar gnawing pain would afflict me years later, with the recognition of a love that could neither be mentioned nor properly gratified – a love, paradoxically, that has sustained me for twenty-five years of solitude.

Here I was, in London, safely delivered by the French guard – who gained a small fortune in English money from my smiling uncle – looking about me, bewildered.

— You will be Andrew, Andrei. Andrew. For all the time you are in my care.

I was still in his arms. He was bearing me out of the station and into the chauffeur-driven car that was waiting for us.

— This is my nephew, he said to the driver in the new language I would soon be learning.

— Welcome to England, Andrew. My uncle translated Charlie's greeting, and instructed me to say
thank you, which I somehow did.

— Thank you. My first new words on that first
evening.

I had never been in a lift, because we had no such
modern thing in our town, but here I was, with my
uncle's hand on my shoulder, going up and up to his
apartment on the top floor of Nightingale Mansions.
That lift would become a golden cage in which I was
happy to be imprisoned. I loved the way it clanked to
a stop. In summer, when most of the Nightingale's
residents were on holiday in the south of France, I
lived in my cage whenever I was free to play, working
the magic handle that set it in motion, jumping in and
out of it as the mood took me.

I heard the clanking sound for the first time that
evening, and then here I was entering my uncle
Rudolf's London home. I was hugged and kissed by
Annie, his housekeeper, who smelt of a soap I would
discover was called carbolic, and who whispered
Andrew, Andrew, over and over again, into my ear.

— You poor, lovely boy, she was saying, you poor,
lovely boy. I heard affection in her voice, but with no
knowledge of what she was really telling me. Annie

would say to me later, as she poured porridge into my special bowl, that I was her poor, lovely boy from the moment she saw me on that cold February night. I was her clever boy, too, for speaking English so well.

My uncle's flat was sumptuous. The word was unknown to me in 1937, for I had not been raised in anything like luxury. My parents had had no cause to use it, ever. *Somptuos*. Our house in the small country town – the house I was expecting to live in again – was humble, and humbly furnished. But Uncle Rudolf's furniture was of a kind I could not even dream of, and had no words to describe until I became the English nephew he wanted me to be. Although I was tired and confused, my eyes took in the vast sofa, the shining mahogany table, the chaise longue, the grand piano, the chandelier, and the paintings and drawings that covered every wall. I gawped. I gawped in wonder, in utter astonishment.

I slept alongside my uncle that night. He sang me to sleep with a lullaby.

— Annie burns the toast to perfection, said Uncle Rudolf in the old language. I have trained her well.

It was at breakfast, on my third day in England, that he announced he had to visit Paris. Urgent business. A chance to sing, perhaps, at the Opéra. He wished he could take me with him, but it would not be fun for me, waiting in some lonely hotel room for an uncle who was engaged elsewhere. Annie and Teddy would keep me amused, and Charlie would drive me around London, showing me all of the sights, and he would call me on the telephone, speaking the words we both understood. I was not to be worried or upset. He would be back with me by Friday, at the very latest. I was in safe hands.

Those safe hands were Annie's, Teddy's and Charlie's – my uncle's doting servants. I sat in the kitchen with the perspiring Annie, watching as she prepared the food that was so different from anything Mamă had cooked for me; and I walked with Teddy Grubb to the bank that was proud to have Rudolf Peterson's custom, and where I was given a freshly minted pound note by the cashier, and then I was Charlie's happy passenger for an entire rainy afternoon, seeing nothing of the promised sights but revelling in the fact – the unlikely fact – that I was in a car the like of which the people in our town would not have believed existed.

I rode in state that day, I realize, and innumerable times after. The Debt Collector's grandson might have been a prince, to look at him.

What I remember – what I cannot fail to remember in the light of what I was to learn – of that first telephone conversation with my uncle is that he did not tell me the truth. It was part of his deceitful plan to save me for as long as possible from griefs I was too young to bear. He sounded buoyant as he told me he had been in the company of a beautiful woman. Paris was the place for beautiful women.

He brought me back a souvenir. It was a model of the Eiffel Tower, from the top of which, thirteen years later, he and I would survey the city he had arrived in thirty years earlier with the intention of becoming the finest lyric tenor in the world.

My pen is darting across these pages, yet I fear he will elude me, the last and most substantial of my three dear ghosts. 'My pen'; 'these pages' – how quaint I must seem, how moribund, in this age of spectacularly advanced technology. But the pen and pages are appropriate since I am writing of the Rudolf Peterson his public would not have understood, or even applauded, in those vanished years of his immense fame. The music he sang deals only fleetingly with sorrow, but sorrow was of my uncle's essence, and it encompassed more than his own fierce melancholy, as I came to understand. To begin with, I noticed that sorrow only in glimpses. I would enter a room – in London, or in Sussex – and he would be unaware of my silent presence. He was often staring ahead of him, contemplating something painful, I guessed, to judge by the look of blankness on his normally lively features. Then, seeing me, he would lose the discontented expression in an instant and start chatting to his beloved nephew of everyday concerns, such as the surprise dish he had asked Annie to prepare for supper. With Andrew to entertain and interest, it seemed, there was no call for sadness.

The voice you can hear today on the Golden Age label gives just a hint of what he was about. It is bright and confident, as befits a reckless vagabond; a prince who believes he is a simple gypsy fiddler; a champagne-guzzling gambler who plays roulette with no thought of a ruinous tomorrow. These were the kind of improbable men Uncle Rudolf impersonated, giving them – for as long as he could bear to – angelic expression. But the angel wanted to sing of other matters; of other, more serious, concerns, and he had already left it too late to do so by the time I arrived in his life.

— You are my mascot, my lucky charm, my uncle said as I watched his face in the dressing-room mirror being transformed into that of Zoltan Kassák, the brigand with whom the Crown Princess Zelda falls at first hopelessly, and then triumphantly, in love. Zoltan has a duelling scar on his left cheek, which Uncle Rudolf created each night with a strip of blood-red plasticine stuck on with theatrical glue.

— It mustn't look too livid, he told me as he dabbed it with powder. Zelda has to find it irresistible.

As Zoltan, my uncle wore immensely baggy trousers that billowed above his leather boots. His brigand's clothes also included an embroidered shirt and a cap from which protruded an eagle's feather. The sword and dagger hanging from his belt proclaimed him to be a man who would fight his enemies to the death, should it be necessary. I can remember, now, watching from the side of the stage as he roused his fellow brigands into action with the song 'What fear we of the foe?' and marvelling that I was

there, on that summer evening, to bring him luck. I
stood, entranced, throughout the first performance
of *Magyar Maytime*, though I was confused by the
story, and still am, if I think about it. In the last
scene, Zoltan is discovered to have noble blood, and
this means that Zelda, who is forbidden to marry a
commoner, can become his bride. My uncle loathed
the coy badinage – 'You are my lovely, my wonderful
Zelly'; 'You are my handsome Zolly, who is so brave
and strong' – that preceded the duet in which they
declare eternal love for one another. His leading lady
was equally embarrassed at having to call him Zolly,
and sometimes he substituted 'smelly' or 'belly' or
'jelly', and she 'folly' or 'dolly' or 'Molly', and then
they would giggle, and the angry conductor in the
pit would be forced to wait for them to stop before
raising his baton.

   — It is a silly life I lead, Andrew. Yours will be
more sensible I hope. And happier.

My mother was with me briefly today – speaking the
only words she knew – in those moments between
sleeping and waking. She said what was true, that she
had never left me, although we had been parted.

   — No parting, Andrei, was more terrible than

ours. Her ghost's voice was as light and soft as the voice that had soothed and comforted and teased me in my earliest years. She told me that her God was the same kind and merciful God she had taught me to believe in but whom I have since abandoned, and then the voice was gone, and the blurred vision of her young face, and I was on the verge of talking to her when I realized that I was awake and alone and shivering in the warmth of the afternoon.

— I have a confession to make, Andrew. Your father and I were rivals for your mother's affections. Irina preferred Roman. If she had chosen me, I would not be enjoying my nephew's company. On balance, I suppose I should be glad she threw me over.

— Were you in love with Mamă, Uncle?

— Very much. She was so serious and shy. She wasn't – as they say here – *forward*.

I knew by then, though I had been given no reason why, that I would not, could not, see her again. I was fifteen by now, and the war with Germany was almost over. My uncle looked older, with white hairs on his temples he made no attempt to disguise. He was in a melancholy mood, a mood to which I was already happily accustomed.

— I try not to dwell on the past, Andrew. It's over,
I remind myself. What's done cannot be undone.
The present is all that matters. Remember that, if
you can. As for me these days, I tend to forget
it. Irina decided wisely when she picked Roman.
I offered them money, my Vienna money, to get
out of that beastly country – our beastly country,
Andrew – but they refused to accept it. I should
have gone to Botoșani and bullied them into leaving.

I asked him why.

I was trapped in his fierce brown stare for a
moment.

— Oh, it was no place for good people. He added,
mysteriously: But you are my future, Andrew. That's
why. Whatever happens, I shall always be at your side
when you need me. Yes, you are my future, for the
time being.

Perhaps he had considered telling me the real
reason why on that April day in 1945, and had then
– in the course of staring at me – persuaded himself
that a boy of fifteen was too raw for such knowledge.
Perhaps.

He suggested that we take a walk in the fields.
There was no danger any more from German planes.

The lord of the manor, as he mockingly described himself, would inspect the estate with his heir apparent.

We ate an omelette that evening, cooked with the fresh eggs his hens had laid.

— What luxury. What a simple luxury, said my smiling uncle. We are very fortunate.

I was to receive the real reason why, the real answer to my question, when I was eighteen.

— You are mature for your age, Andrew. I will pour you a large brandy before I say what I have to say. I certainly need one.

What he told me on the tenth of August, 1948, caused me to shiver today.

I remember that I needed a second large brandy after I had read my father's last letter to my uncle, written in the old words I no longer spoke.

The words that are ashes in my mouth when I catch myself speaking them now.

— We shall have an English Christmas, not an Orthodox one. Santa Claus will come down the chimney with your presents. He's like Saint Nicholas only different, as they say here. You must sleep tight, my dear, because Santa doesn't want you to see him being kind. Do you promise me you won't try to look at him?

— I promise, Uncle.

It was December 1937, and I was still in England, on holiday. We were at Uncle Rudolf's Elizabethan house in the Sussex countryside, with his devoted entourage – Annie, Teddy and Charlie – whom he now instructed me not to call his servants.

— They are my friends, Andrew darling. They work for me, yes, but on the best of terms. They are our equals, not inferiors.

(Yet the girls Annie ruled over with a steely eye for any slipshod cleaning or polishing or bed-making were obviously there as unobtrusive servants, fulfilling necessary chores.)

Annie, Teddy and Charlie were a privileged trio, and they basked in that privilege. The widowed Annie, the divorced Teddy and Charlie, the dedicated 'bit of a skirt-chaser' – a phrase I learned from Charlie's lips even before my English lessons began in earnest – regarded their friendly employer as a very paragon.

I kept my promise to sleep tight. Uncle Rudolf had ensured that I would, by having dinner served late on Christmas Eve. It might have been the sherry in the trifle and the half-glass of champagne I was advised to sip that made me drowsy, but I was definitely 'on the way to the Land of Nod' – as Annie often joked – when my uncle carried me upstairs to bed. And what delights awaited me that Christmas morning, delivered to my little room with such amazing stealth: a train set, complete with signals and stations, with miniature porters and passengers and a beaming driver at the helm; a huge wooden jigsaw puzzle of the Houses of Parliament; sheets of drawing paper, with coloured pencils and crayons; *Babar the Elephant* in French, and an English dictionary, my first and most beloved, that would, as Uncle Rudolf predicted, bring me not only a new language but a whole new world. These are the gifts, the precious gifts, I remember today, but I think there were others to unwrap beneath my uncle's adoring gaze.

My playmate, if the term is appropriate, that Christmas was Maurice, the ten-year-old son of Charlie and a skirt he had chased successfully. Maurice was bored and morose in my company, though I did reduce him to jeering laughter whenever I attempted to speak a snatch or two of English.

— You sound funny. Your uncle doesn't, but you do. You don't know how funny you sound.

But otherwise Maurice glowered at me – yes, glowered is right – during our playtime. I suppose, now, that he felt too grown-up in my childish presence, too preoccupied with the fact that his parents, Charlie and Edith, were not united in either love or marriage. He had no family, as I had. That may be my old man's fancy, set down with all the confidence of hindsight, but Maurice, coming home on leave from Malta would try, and fail, to kill his mother ten years later. The young sailor had found her with a stranger, naked on the kitchen table. The man, a respected doctor, dressed in haste while Maurice glowered at him, I imagine, as he had once glowered at me. Alone with Edith, who was offering excuses for her behaviour, Maurice picked up a knife and stabbed her in the arm, the shoulder and, most dangerously, the chest. It was the contrite Maurice who summoned the police. His mother survived, after an emergency operation that lasted several hours. Maurice stood trial, in 1948, for attempted murder, and was found guilty, but with extenuating circumstances. The defending counsel depicted Edith as the loosest type of loose woman, and a Sunday newspaper named her the Finchley Jezebel. Maurice was sent to prison, where he shortly died.

Maurice's laughter as he scorned my feeble English wasn't happily full-throated. I know that I sensed the strain in it. We were always uneasy together, and grateful when Annie or Charlie or Uncle Rudolf appeared with cake and jellies and chocolate. We both needed those cheerful adults to be with us, and for subtly different reasons, it occurs to me. I can express today what I couldn't then, even in the old words – that, seeing a few snowflakes fall, my heart was suddenly in my throat. As the flakes fell and almost instantly evaporated, I had a vision of the wonderful carpet I had walked on the previous December, hand-in-hand with Tată. I thought, too, of Mamă ordering me away from the window, to eat – what was it I ate? – the pie she had baked with cașcavel cheese, which comes from ewe's milk, and mushrooms.

My uncle hosted a supper party that Christmas evening. I wore a tailored suit with short trousers, a crisp white shirt and a black bow tie.

— Andrew is the guest of honour, he announced as each of his guests arrived. My nephew, my darling *nipote*.

Uncle Rudolf raised me aloft to shake hands with a famous actor, a famous prima donna (who kissed me on both cheeks), a famous theatrical designer, another famous actor and his famous actress wife, a famous cabaret singer, a famous playwright and a pianist who wasn't as famous as he deserved to be. Among all these famous or not-so-famous people, I was the guest of honour, my uncle insisted. He sat me next to him, at the head of the dining table.

We ate by candlelight. No, *they* ate by candlelight, while I nibbled, nothing more, at the strange food that was set in front of me. The meal was served by the always-perspiring Annie with the aid of two girls from the village, who mumbled 'Beg pardon, sir' and 'Beg pardon, madam' until Uncle Rudolf ordered them, politely, to stop. It was Annie who noticed my reluctance to touch the dark meat on my plate, and it was she who removed the partridge breast and the pear stewed in red wine, scolding Mr Rudolf for expecting her poor, lovely boy to eat such a rich dish. I was given some Brussels sprouts and a roast potato, cut into small pieces, and felt less discomfort.

The wines were poured by Teddy Grubb, who was said to 'have a nose' for them. In later years, my uncle would tease me for saying 'Mr Grubb has a nose' before I had even mastered the alphabet. The faces of the famous became redder and livelier as the supper progressed. They cheered when Annie brought in the Christmas pudding, which Uncle Rudolf doused in brandy. Someone shouted 'Whoosh' when he put a match to it, sending flames rising. I was afraid the flames would spread and that we would all be burnt, but they soon subsided, to everyone's applause.

— Clap your hands, Andrew. It's the custom.

Everyone clapped again when I discovered a bright new shilling in my slice of pudding. I had to lick it clean of custard to appreciate its brightness.

— That's a sign you'll be wealthy one day. As you will be, I promise.

My uncle stood up and asked for silence. Conversation and laughter slowly drifted away.

— I should like us to drink a toast to absent friends.

He patted me on the head as the famous guests rose and said, almost in unison:

— Absent friends.

Did I realize that I was the object of pitying looks? I think I must have done, for the eyes of everybody in the dining room were suddenly focused on me.

— To all our dear ones.

— To all our dear ones.

— To those who are with us.

— To those who are with us.

— And to those who have been taken from us.

There was a hush. No one responded to this toast, as they had responded to the others. I waited to hear them repeat 'And to those who have been taken from us' but the hush prevailed. Uncle Rudolf told me, some years on, that I wriggled in my chair and blushed with embarrassment, to have so many kind and thoughtful eyes fixed upon me that night.

— Now let's be happy again.

After the ladies had 'powdered their noses' and the gentlemen had smoked their cigarettes and cigars, the Christmas party took place in the drawing room. I sat on the famous prima donna's knee and watched the adults play charades. I was, of course, mystified. Maurice, who had not eaten supper with us, was invited to join in. One of his few boasts would be that for three Christmasses he had acted with two of the most famous actors in the theatre, thanks to the fact that his dad was Rudolf Peterson's personal driver.

It is the not-so-famous pianist I remember best, simply because he was my uncle's regular accompanist. His name was Ivan, but he wasn't Russian. Uncle Rudolf called him Ivan the Terrible whenever he hit a wrong note or was out of time. The prima donna refused to sing that first Christmas and the cabaret artist was so drunk that he forgot his words, to everyone's amusement, and so it was that my uncle, who was not sober, beckoned Ivan Morris over to the piano.

— You must forget Danilo, and the Gypsy Baron, and the Vagabond King, and that bloody idiot of a brigand Zoltan, and all the other halfwits in my repertoire.

My uncle cleared his throat, signalled to Ivan that he was ready to begin, and then sang the aria from Handel's *Jephtha* in which the anguished father offers up his only child for sacrifice:

> *Waft her, angels, through the skies,*
> *Far above yon azure plain;*
> *Glorious there, like you, to rise,*
> *There, like you, for ever reign.*

I was unaware of Jephtha's plight, and I had never heard Handel's music before, but I did understand, at the age of seven, that I had just listened to something radiantly beautiful.

On a fine morning in November 1919, my uncle went

to the top of the Eiffel Tower and looked down on the city.

— It wasn't only Paris I was seeing, Andrew. I had the world in my sights. I was young and glowing with confidence. I really believed what my teacher in Botoşani had told me – that my voice was a gift from God. When you have God as your benefactor, my darling, you don't have any doubts.

Uncle Rudolf walked the streets of Paris for most of that day, speaking French whenever he could. He stopped for lunch at a bistro, where he ate cassoulet and drank, such was the state of excitement he was in, an entire bottle of claret. When he boarded the night train for Nice, he was in a mood to sleep, but his by now highly-charged nerves would allow him no rest. Towards the end of the eighteen-hour journey – tired, and with dust in his eyes and throat – he began to wonder if God, who had been his inspiration and ally in Botoşani and at the Conservatoire in Bucharest, might now be abandoning him, relegating him to the ranks of mere mortals. It was an anxious Rudi Petrescu who stood on the platform at Nice, wondering for a terrified moment if he should return to Paris, and thence to the country in which God had not deserted him. But some hope, a residue of the confidence he had enjoyed at the top of the Eiffel Tower, spurred him on, pushed him – so to speak – in the direction of the little *pension* where he had a room reserved indefinitely. The *pension*'s owner, Mme Barrière, inspected him through pince-nez, and let out a noise indicative of her approval of his looks. She was fifty, perhaps, and gone to fat, but he was seduced, quite literally, by her charm. They made love in his room – quickly, passionately – for the one and only time. From then on, he was her 'pretty Romanian boy'; her *fils*, even.

— Whenever she called me her son, I felt rather like Oedipus. She became really motherly after our – how shall I say? – *rencontre brève et violente*.

Thanks to his exertions with the buxom landlady, my uncle was able to sleep at last. The following morning, his anxiety returned. He was conscious, as he got out of bed, that his heart was beating unusually fast and that his hands were shaking. He would have to calm down somehow. Disaster loomed. He rang for the maid to bring him a jug of hot water. He needed to shave with especial care on this, the most important day in his life so far. In two hours – less, a glance at his fob watch confirmed – he would be shown into the presence of the greatest operatic tenor of the nineteenth century, who was now the doyen of singing teachers. While he was thinking of his extraordinary good fortune – he could always claim he had met Jean de Reszke, whatever the outcome of today's meeting – he cut himself on the chin. He tried to still the flow of blood with a towel pressed tight against it, but as soon as he took the towel away the blood trickled out once more. He tore off a strip of writing paper and applied it to the offending spot, pressing and pressing until his patience cracked. He looked in the mirror above the wash basin and as he did so the blood started to spurt again. He was in a panic; he was desperate. He applied another strip of paper to his chin and left it sticking there as he washed and dressed. He combed his hair and dabbed cologne on his cheeks and ears.

He drank coffee and a glass of chilled water at a bar before setting off for the Villa Vergemère. He strolled along the Promenade des Anglais, counting each palm tree he passed in order to keep his mind distracted. The day was already warm and he feared he might begin to sweat if he walked at a brisker pace. He turned into the avenue leading up to the villa and realized he had sung nothing since waking up. A ridiculous sense of embarrassment – ridiculous because he was totally alone – prevented him from practising his scales as he moved ever closer to his destiny.

— Yes, Andrew, my destiny. That was what was about to be decided.

At last the villa came into view. Poplars as well as palms lined the approach to it. Although it was November, there were roses in bloom. He paused for a moment and saw the Mediterranean glittering below. He was in paradise. If his nerves would only cease tormenting him, he was in a paradise on earth, he thought. He continued to climb, because Jean de Reszke's villa was on the very peak of the hill. The gates were open and he entered the driveway. A man was standing on the steps leading up to the Villa Vergemère with a hand outstretched to welcome him.

— You will be Monsieur Petrescu?

My uncle answered, in French, that he was.

— I am Louis Vachet, the master's secretary and valet. You have something attached to your face. A piece of paper, is it not?

— Yes, Monsient Vachet. I cut myself shaving.

— Do you wish to remove it?

— Of course.

— Give it to me. I will dispose of it for you.

The smiling Louis Vachet took the blood-stopper from him with the words:

— You were nervous, I expect. The master will put you at your ease. Follow me, Monsieur Petrescu.

Uncle Rudolf remembered that the Great Hall of the Villa Vergemère merited its name. It was as long as it was wide and the ceiling seemed impossibly high.

— You are his only pupil this morning, Monsieur Petrescu. You are honoured.

— Yes, Monsieur Vachet.

— Do not be disconcerted by Koko, Louis Vachet remarked mysteriously, opening the door of an enormous room, into which he almost had to push my awestruck uncle.

The tall man who stood by the window overlooking the sea bore little resemblance to the one disguised as Faust and Tristan in the photographs Uncle Rudolf had studied. This Jean de Reszke was bald – though he still had a moustache, neatly trimmed and less voluminous than Tristan's or Faust's or Romeo's – and noticeably fat, with a paunch his elegantly-fitted suit emphasized rather than hid. A green parrot was perched on his right shoulder. This, it was clear, was the disconcerting Koko.

— May I present Monsieur Petrescu, Master?

Jean de Reszke smiled at the trembling Monsieur Petrescu, nodded, and said:

— Sing.

God has gone from me, thought my uncle. Here I am with a parched throat and lungs clogged up with the dust of Nice.

— Sing? he heard himself ask, to his immediate shame.

— Yes, monsieur. It is a natural request. You wish to become a singer, do you not? Sing for me, if you will. *A cappella.*

Dalla sua pace la mia dipende

Rudi Petrescu sang, croakily. Koko screeched, and Jean de Reszke commanded him to stop.

— Don Ottavio must wait, Monsieur Petrescu. You are not prepared for him. He will be there when you are. Sing me a song. Forget opera for the moment.

It was then that my uncle sang the Romanian folk song his first teacher, Cezar Avădanei, had heard him sing five years earlier. A Carpathian shepherd is sighing for love of the beautiful girl found dead in the winter snow. His sheep cannot tell that his heart is for ever broken.

— *Bien*, said Jean de Reszke when he had finished.

— *Bien* is my favourite word in any language, Andrew. De Reszke was not the man for lavish praise. His *bien* told you what you wanted to hear from him. On the days he said *bien*, I left Villa Vergemère in a state of happiness that had no limits. All was well for me.

— It would seem that Monsieur Georges Enesco is correct in his judgement of your singing ability. He wrote me a letter recommending you as a pupil.

— I sang for him in Bucharest, Master. At the Conservatoire.

(How easily, how naturally, that Master, that *Maître*, had come to him.)

— I know of his skills as a violinist. He is a composer also, I believe. I should imagine that his music is too modern, too *new*, for my old ears. Do you have money, Monsieur Petrescu?

— Not very much, Master.

— I am not asking out of avarice. Let us be practical. Can you afford to remain in Nice for, shall we say, six months?

— No, Master.

— That is a problem – a purely financial problem – we shall have to solve.

It was solved by Jean de Reszke quietly and discreetly, with Mme Barrière informing my uncle that his bill had been paid as far ahead as May. At Christmas, Louis Vachet handed him an envelope containing a small present from the master.

— Three thousand francs, Andrew. It was a fortune.

The lessons began each morning at nine precisely. The master descended the stairs, his paunch preceding him, with Koko on his shoulder.

— He spoke in French, and very occasionally said something in his native Polish, but there was one English word, and one only, that he loved. It was 'belly'. He would pat his stomach and say '*Mon* belly' and then he'd laugh out loud. '*Mon* belly, Monsieur Petrescu. *C'est énorme.*'

He taught my uncle not to declaim, because he considered declaiming unnatural. In the real world, preachers and politicians declaim, but ordinary people converse. He advised him to cultivate a love of the word – '*l'amour de la parole*' – since singing is not concerned with music alone. A beautiful noise is merely a beautiful noise. And he reminded him that human feelings are subtle and varied and should be afforded subtle and varied expression. He had never wept on stage, nothing so *vulgar*, but he had made audiences weep, in all modesty, by shading his voice with sadness or melancholy or sorrow.

— It is common to think that tenors are stupid, Monsieur Petrescu. That they have a vacant space where their brains should be. And out of that vacant space emerges the lovely tenor sound. You must prove the cynics wrong, as I once did. I sang with my head *and* my brains, as you must do. Your head notes are good, but you have intelligence also. Give me the opportunity to appreciate both.

Uncle Rudolf often spoke wistfully of the days he spent at the villa, of the purple clematis and yellow mimosa blossoming in abundance that spring. He chuckled at the memory of Koko's screech, which he first mimicked for me while I was still a little boy. He was at his most eloquent, however, when he talked of Jean de Reszke's gentlemanly reticence in the face of suffering. The sweet-tempered perfectionist was in mourning for his beloved brother, Edouard, the great bass baritone – the Mephistopheles to his Faust; the Frère Laurent to his Romeo – who had died in

1916, and for his only son, Jean, who was killed by a stray bullet in Flanders in June 1918, after surviving the battle of the Marne. These were private griefs, not to be shared with his pupils, of whom M. Petrescu was the one the master had singled out for a more-than-promising future.

Life at Villa Vergemère was largely peaceful and productive, with the master receiving loving support from Louis Vachet, and the American musicologist Amherst Webber, who frequently and patiently accompanied his students at the piano, and from his niece Minia, who adored him as her second father. Rudi Petrescu was at ease with them, and they with him, for they sensed that he was fired by the proper kind of ambition. In those classes, and there were many, when the master did not feel compelled to say *bien*, the young Romanian did not sulk or fret, as others had. He persevered, as he was meant to do, with the task the master set him. It was the simplest of tasks, and yet the most difficult – to give each word in a song or aria its necessary meaning. There was a French sound, and a German sound, and an Italian sound, and M. Petrescu – the formality of this manner of addressing him did not exclude warmth – must learn, as he had learnt, how to make himself French

or German or Italian and not with sound alone. M.
Petrescu was to follow the example of actors, who had
no music to hide behind. He was to imagine he was
speaking what he was, in fact, singing.

There was one person in the villa, one very important person, who did not care for M. Petrescu. He,
in turn, did not understand why she treated him with
such sustained animosity. It was Mme de Reszke's
habit to appear out of nowhere, in a room that
seemed to be solely occupied by the master, the
pianist and the pupil. She would emerge from behind
an unoccupied chair – had she been crouching like
a cat, ready to pounce on her prey? – with a cry of
'*Toujours les élèves*' and then storm out, banging the
door loudly. She cared for none of the students, it was
true, but only Rudi Petrescu inspired her to be openly
vindictive. Sometimes she was rendered speechless
in his presence, shaking an angry fist in his direction,
as if to compensate for the insult she was unable to
hurl at him.

It was the tactful Louis Vachet who offered him an
explanation for her curious behaviour. M. Petrescu
must understand that Madame had been gravely
upset by the death of her son. So had the master,
of course, but it was in his nature to be stoical –

on the surface, at least. On receiving the terrible
news, Madame had become hysterical, completely
and utterly hysterical. Doctors were called in to
tend to her. There was a fear, a genuine fear on
the master's part, that she might have gone mad.
One of the doctors had even suggested that Madame
might be placed in an institution, so alarming were
the symptoms she was displaying. But that solution,
if solution it was, had been averted, thanks be to God,
and Madame was now on the way to recovery. She
had not been happy with the master's decision to
move from Paris to Nice, and she was not pleased
he had resumed his career as a teacher. She was
uncomfortable in the company of youth. It was not
M. Petrescu himself who caused her to be impolite, it
was the very fact of his youthfulness. M. Jean had died
young, in an absurd circumstance, and M. Petrescu
was alive. M. Jean had been a talented painter, and
M. Petrescu was a talented singer and her husband's
protégé.

— Try not to be too disturbed by Madame. Consider what I have told you, Monsieur Petrescu, and
stay calm, if that is possible.

When Uncle Rudolf heard, a few years later,
that Madame de Reszke had not been with the

master as he was dying – Minia was with him, and Louis Vachet, and Amherst Webber – he was confirmed in his suspicion that theirs had been a loveless marriage. Jean had wanted to marry Natalie Potocka and she him, but her nobleman father would not countenance a union between his daughter and a man who appeared on the stage in public. Natalie and Jean were to meet at intervals, and on each occasion it was pitifully clear to both of them their love for each other hadn't waned. Natalie would die unmarried.

Rudi Petrescu was grateful for those days at the villa when Madame wasn't lurking behind the furniture; when he could sing the Flower Song from *Carmen* with only the consummate Don José of the 1890s to interrupt him. And Koko, too. How could he possibly forget or ignore Koko, his sharpest, loudest critic? The master guided him through the Flower Song – word by word; note by note – for the entire month of February, on the very last day of which he received a *bien* so fulsome and generous that he nearly wept.

— I did weep, actually, Andrew darling. On the Promenade des Anglais. I stopped walking and cried for joy.

Jean de Reszke was beaming at him when he

arrived for his class at nine o'clock precisely on the fourth of March, 1920.

— You have a visitor, Monsieur Petrescu.

— Where, Master? asked my uncle, seeing no one else in the room.

— Go to the piano.

He did as instructed and found the score of *Don Giovanni* opened at *Dalla sua pace.*

— Don Ottavio is your visitor. He has been absent since last November, when you had the impertinence to sing on his behalf. He took offence and vanished. He has returned in a more optimistic frame of mind.

— Do you think he will stay, Master?

— We shall endeavour, between us, to persuade him to do so.

And persuade him they did, over six long weeks compounded in equal measure of frustration and enlightenment. *Bien* remained unspoken. Koko screeched twice, though not on the same day. A whole morning was devoted – and devoted it was, in the highest sense, my uncle acknowledged – to the phrase *morte mi dà.*

In June 1920, Rudi Petrescu appeared as Don Ottavio in a student production of *Don Giovanni* in

a small opera house in Nice. He was the one member
of the cast to achieve fame.

In my waking hours I was Andrew, because that was
what everyone called me. I was Andrew as I dutifully
munched burnt toast at breakfast and I was still
Andrew when Annie bathed me and helped me into
my pyjamas and tucked me up in bed. It was Andrew
who listened to stories about giants and goblins and
animals who talked like people, and it was as Andrew
that I fell asleep. My bedroom door would be left
ajar, with a chink of light coming from the passage
to remind me I was in a safe place.

In dreams I became Andrei again, as often as
not, running across the wonderful carpet in search
of Mamă and Tată, whose backs I could make out
somewhere in the far distance. Why did they never
stop for me? I shouted after them. I am Andrei; I
screamed, I am Andrei, your son. But they never
turned to look at me, and they kept on walking away,
further and further away, until even the sight of their
backs was denied me. I was blinded by whiteness.

The Andrei I became in dreams was not always the
same happy Andrei who had clutched his mother's
skirts and marvelled at the pictures in his father's

magazine. This Andrei was not to be comforted by his parents, who were either walking away from him or frighteningly absent. The cabbage soup he tried to eat in the snow had frozen over, and the spoon in his hand was unable to crack its surface. The Virgin in the icon came to cackling life, dropping the baby Jesus at his feet. The holy child broke into tiny pieces, as if he were a doll, and it proved impossible to put him together again. The pieces were resistant to Andrei's touch.

— That's the Debt Collector's daughter (sneered the woman in the market) striking a hard bargain.

And then I heard my mother's sobs, and awoke with my own.

— There, there, my darling, whispered my uncle, retrieving me from the sheet in which I was entangled. You are here with me, in London. No harm will come to you, I promise. Your uncle loves you, my little angel.

He lifted me up in his arms and carried me to his bedroom, where he set me down on his vast double bed. He took off his dressing-gown and lay beside me.

— Let me cuddle you to sleep.

I was living between two languages, the old words

and the new. At the age of eight, as I was soon to be, I was not in possession of a vocabulary that could encompass either Andrew's feelings of wonderment or Andrei's confusion at having been abandoned. There were times during the day when the wondering Andrew would be seized by a numb, wordless despair that had to be Andrei's, so blindingly white was it, so redolent of the snow that transformed the huts of peasants into igloos. It was Andrew, not Andrei, who asked his uncle to please sing *Waft her, angels*, as his special present on his eighth birthday, and it would be Andrew who requested it again and again, until Uncle Rudolf – bored at last – sang *Dalla sua pace* for him, as he had once sung it in the enormous room at Villa Vergemère, with its view of the Mediterranean, for the fastidious and demanding Jean de Reszke.

The dreams persisted, with the helpless, lost Andrei for ever in pursuit of his departing parents. The Virgin Mary scoffed, and the infant Jesus – the saviour of my mother's world – was so many shards of china or clay. Sometimes the woman in the market kept her peace, and sometimes she didn't. Then the old woodman Mircea said *Wickedness, wickedness* as he had done that icy morning when Tată and I had fled the town, and then one night his ancient horse was there, clouding the air with his foul breath, and opening his yellow mouth wider and wider the better to gobble me up. My head was in the grip of his rotting teeth when the chink of light from the passage came to remind the screaming Andrew that all was safe.

Uncle Rudolf removed my pyjamas, which were damp with the chill sweat of terror, and lowered me gently into his bed. It was a very hot summer night. I was naked now, and so was he, and as I lay enfolded in his hairy embrace, I felt comforted and calmed. My protector: I knew that's what he was long before the word was mine to use. When I slept alongside him, I was the Andrew he had deemed me to be, the nephew he had chosen to protect. Protect me from what? He would tell me, in time, of the legal problems he had had to combat and overcome in order to keep me with him in England – the documents he'd had to sign; the endless wrangling with solicitors and lawyers. It had been his impossible task to explain to those blinkered individuals, whose knowledge of the Europe beyond their shores was restricted to French accordion players and onion sellers, Germans in lederhosen eating sauerkraut, and lecherous Italians consuming ice cream, that the country of his birth was not a suitable place for a sensitive boy to be raised in. The orphaned Andrei Petrescu had no future, no civilized future, there. How could he have? He implored them to consider the reason why he had brought the child to London and safety. He talked of the forest, and of Roman Petrescu's decision to extricate himself from a life that was unendurable.

There was a night, not to be forgotten, when Andrei ran after his Mamă and Tată, when the Virgin cackled and Jesus fell out of the icon and smashed into fragments, when the woman in the market was at her nastiest, and when his mother's tears became the waking Andrew's, that I was taken up and borne to my uncle's bedroom. My boy's body was still wracked with sobbing as I realized that the bed was occupied by someone else – a blonde woman I had never met and, as it transpired, would not meet again.

— Andrew has had a bad dream, Sylvia.

— Oh, the poor thing.

— I shall hug him for a little while, and then he'll fall asleep. It always does the trick.

His hugs didn't do the trick on this one occasion, I remember, because I was curious, in the way children are curious, to learn more about this Sylvia, smoking a cigarette through a long holder. Wrapped in Uncle Rudolf's arms, I feigned sleep and listened.

— Was that the last rubber johnny?

— No.

— You're well stocked, are you? Keep a supply of them, do you?

— That's right, Sylvia.

— Prepared for every emergency, are you?

— Exactly.

— Is what's-his-name asleep?

— Andrew. He seems to be.

— Get a fresh johnny then.

— I can't. I can't take the risk.

— We were having fun before cry-baby started bawling.

— He's twelve years old. He's not a baby.

— You could bring me off with your fingers.

— I could and I couldn't. Charlie will drive you back to London.

— You bastard.

— A generous bastard, Sylvia. You won't have to suffer the discomfort of the milk train. I shall call for Charlie while you're washing and dressing.

Uncle Rudolf was startled to learn during breakfast that I had overheard his conversation with Sylvia.

— How much of it did you understand, you scamp?

Not the rubber johnny and not the fingers, I replied. Thus it was that I received my first, thorough lesson on the facts of life. He did not talk of birds and bees. He said that a 'rubber johnny' was a contraceptive. He showed me one from his stock. Men wore them to prevent their girlfriends or wives becoming pregnant. And as for the finger or fingers – they had often saved the sexual day for him when his penis had been unwilling to function. I would discover more for myself, by and by, and with pleasure, he hoped, and with love.

— I suppose you have Sylvia to thank for your new-found knowledge.

Another kind of knowledge was imparted to me, the unmistakably English Andrew, some months after my eighteenth birthday. As a result of what Uncle Rudolf revealed to me – slowly, haltingly, over large, medicinal brandies – Andrei gave up the vain pursuit of his Mamă and Tată; the family's icon remained intact; Mircea's horse's mouth no more than yawned, but the woman-in-the-market's taunts became louder and fiercer than ever.

❀   ❀   ❀

Uncle Rudolf was joyously happy that *Magyar May-time* turned out to be a disaster. The critics were unanimous in their loathing of it. Not even Mr Rudolf Peterson's undoubted charm and winning way with a melody, one of them wrote, could rescue it from the oblivion it so patently deserved.

— Finely phrased, said my uncle, helping himself to apricot jam. Nicely put. I shall send that discerning gentleman a case of champagne. He deserves nothing less.

In spite of the bad notices, the show ran for longer than anyone had expected. In Act Two, the fearless Zoltan suffered an injury to his leg, and András, his faithful batman and fellow brigand, was required to apply a bandage to the wound. The scene in which my uncle's left calf and knee were exposed while András went about his healing business brought forth cries of ecstasy from the mostly well-bred women in the audience. Some swooned; some actually fainted. There was a ridiculous spectacle one evening when a uniformed nurse vaulted into the orchestra pit, clambered up on to the stage, pushed the actor playing András aside and prostrated herself in front of Zoltan with the words 'I am yours, Rudolf. I am highly trained. Put your faith in Betty.'

— The poor, deluded soul, my uncle would remark whenever he told the story of that extraordinary occasion. They had to drag her, kicking and screaming, off the stage and out of the theatre. And all that for a glimpse of Rudolf Peterson's leg. I hope she came to her senses. I do hope so. I hope she met a sensible man and raised a sensible family and used her highly trained skills to help lots of genuinely wounded people. That's my hope for her in this nonsensical world.

At that time, Uncle Rudolf's jet-black hair, large brown eyes and athlete's physique made a combination that was irresistible to his admirers. Unlike other noted heart-throbs of the age, he had nothing feminine in his appearance. Someone once said that Michelangelo would have found him the perfect model. Uncle Rudolf, recalling this, laughed.

— I know I'm good looking. I would be a liar or a fool if I said I didn't. I often wish that nature had given me a blemish. A flat nose, a non-existent English chin, a baboon's lips.

I was in his dressing room throughout the final performance of *Magyar Maytime* in April 1938.

— You're more like a little boy tonight than that little boy is, said his dresser, pointing at me. I've never seen you in such a skittish mood if I may say so, sir.

— No, you haven't, Joe. Nor is it likely that you ever will again. It's the end of an era for me. The overdue end of an era.

He hugged and kissed me every time he came back to adjust his make-up or change his costume.

— The Rudolf Peterson leg has thrilled the ladies for good. Did you hear the commotion they made, Joe?

— Impossible not to, sir. Like a mob of screaming banshees, or cats on heat.

My uncle had to translate 'banshees' for me, and impersonate the noise a cat makes when it's in the mood for love.

The peculiarly, but not unpleasantly, rancid smell of that dressing room is with me here as I revisit it in memory. It's a smell compounded of other smells – of greasepaint; powder; of my uncle's copious sweat and the cologne (Jicky, I believe it was called) Joe sprayed into his armpits. The strong disinfectant the cleaners used each morning to fumigate ('fumigate' was a new word that delighted me) the theatre is here, too, as it was then.

— The end, the end, the end of an era, Uncle

Rudolf shouted when the last curtain calls had been taken and he was at his dressing table, ruffling his nephew's hair and fidgeting impatiently while Joe undid the buttons on his regal uniform.

— You were my lucky charm, Andrew, as I said you would be. It's over. It's over, my darling. *È finita la commedia*. You are the finest mascot a misguided tenor could have. Thank you, thank you.

His mascot dozed in his uncle's arms during the party he gave at the Ritz to celebrate the end of a personal era. He was saying an unfond farewell to operetta, he announced to cries of 'Shame on you' and 'Think again, Peterson.' He was never more serious. He did not say to his theatrical friends, as he had said to his then-uncomprehending nephew, that he was not too old at thirty-eight to tackle Don Ottavio and Ferrando and have a stab at Don José or Florestan. Time, and impresarios, would tell. There was one great tenor, now in his fifties, who was always singing Otello somewhere in Italy. He, Rudi Petrescu alias Rudolf Peterson, had a certain duty to fulfil.

My uncle was being precipitate. He was to appear in one more operetta, as Igor, the heir to the Boldonian throne, who is enamoured of pretty Mélodie, the servant girl with – yes – royal blood, in *The Gypsy Prince*.

— I am doing it for the money, Andrew, and nothing else. It's all that I'm being offered, anyway.

The critics were dismissive of the show, and cruel to its leading man, who had no leg wound to expose for the benefit of the ladies. It opened in the spring of 1939 and closed in late summer, with the threat of an impending world war causing people to think seriously about the prospect before them. In those dark years, after it was decided he wasn't a threat to national security, he sang for the British troops in Malta and Italy. Then, in December 1945, Uncle Rudolf gave – at his own instigation – a positively fare-well performance at London's most famous variety theatre, the Palladium, in aid of the relatives of those who had perished in Auschwitz, Belsen, Buchenwald and the other concentration camps. He sang from the operettas in which he had made his name in Vienna between 1922 and 1931 – *The Merry Widow*, *The Gypsy Baron* and *Die Fledermaus*. And he sang, as encores, three arias by Mozart, one of which he dedicated to the blessed memory of Jean de Reszke. He ended the evening with the song 'Goodnight, Vienna'.

— Goodnight, Vienna, indeed, he said to the friends and admirers who were crammed into his dressing room. Goodnight and goodbye to the city of cream cakes and Nazi generals. *Güte* shitting *Nacht.*

The train has stopped on the outskirts of Paris, and my father is smoking furiously. Yes, 'furiously' is accurate, for he is lighting one cigarette from another and they are like daggers going in and out of his mouth, I think, because he seems to be stabbing himself with them.

— Nerves, Andrei, he explains, seeing me staring at him. They will pass.

— Do I have to stay with Uncle Rudolf? Do I really have to?

— Yes. For the present. You will come back to me. To *us*.

— When?

— Soon. As soon as possible. You may not want to come back to us. Once you have met Uncle Rudolf, coming back to your Mamă and Tată may be the last thing you want to do.

— Why do you say that, Tată?

— Wait till you meet your uncle, Tată laughs. Of course you will come back to us. Do not look so afraid. Smile for me.

I smile for him because he is my father and he has

asked me to, but I do not want to smile now, not now that the train is moving once more.

— Thank God for that, says Tată, throwing his cigarette out of the window. I was scared you might miss your connection, Andrei. I was nervous for you. With a little luck on our side, we will reach Paris on time.

— Goodness me, said Annie as she opened a brown paper parcel on my uncle's instructions. Whatever can the woman have in mind?

— I shall refrain from answering that question, Annie. We are both well aware what she has in mind.

— I really don't think Andrew should see what's inside.

— Let him see, Annie. Let him be educated in the strange ways of the world. While he eats up his burnt toast, like the good nephew he is.

— It's more ladies' underwear, though whether the floozy who sent you these deserves to be called a lady is another matter.

— She probably has a title, Annie. Is there a note attached to her – what shall we say – gift?

— There is.

— Read it to me. And to Andrew as well, if it isn't too explicit.

— It's quite tame, I have to say, compared to some of them. There aren't any words the boy shouldn't hear. She signs herself Elsie. No, I tell a lie, she doesn't. It's Elise.

— 'Elise' is certainly more romantic than 'Elsie'.

— Romantic is as romantic does, and sending a man your drawers in the post isn't in any romance I've ever read.

— Elise's message, Annie, if you please.

— If you must, Mr Rudolf. 'I dream of you day and night, in and out of the enclosed. Your Elise.'

— That is definitely tame. Bring them forth, Annie. Let Andrew enjoy the spectacle of Elise's under-things.

Annie brought them forth, one by one, with obvious distaste. They were coloured red and white and blue and a hole had been cut into each of them.

— The foul-minded slut.

— But patriotic, Annie. There is no danger of her spying for the Germans, even if her name is Elise.

Uncle Rudolf's shoulders began to heave, and soon his entire body, it seemed, was uncontrollable with laughter.

— You'll be having palpitations, Mr Rudolf, if you carry on like that.

— Oh, Lord, Annie. Oh, Lord. It's just occurred to me that I shan't be able to listen to *Für Elise* again without picturing those patriotic silk panties.

My uncle always relished the disgust Annie exhibited on opening the parcels. Her refined Edinburgh accent became more pronounced and her manner notably prudish, especially when the drawers – as she invariably referred to them – were stained or soiled.

— These are from a Lady Cosgrove, would you believe. Lady Muck's too polite for her. I'd sooner break bread with Lady Macbeth.

Uncle Rudolf and I were intrigued as much as amused by the fact that Annie did not dispose of these 'offending objects' straight away. It was her weird custom, which she refused to account for in terms of logic, to pick up the offending undergarments and bear them at arm's length to the laundry room, where she would deposit them in the huge metal pot in which she boiled tea towels and handkerchiefs. Perhaps she was setting Lady Cosgrove and the other 'hussies', aristocratic or not, an unseen example in cleanliness and decency, or perhaps – my uncle reasoned – she did not want the porter at Nightingale Mansions to come to unpleasant conclusions when he collected the rubbish, even though she had taken care to secrete the newly-fragrant drawers beneath cabbage stalks, potato peelings, cigarette packets, newspapers, tea leaves – the familiar detritus of a busy household.

I witnessed this untoward ritual for many years, until I was old enough to read and comprehend the contents of the letters, notes and cards that accompanied the panties, brassieres and suspender belts my uncle received with startling regularity from his frustrated admirers. He was invited or commanded to sniff them, kiss them, bury his beautiful face in them, wear them, keep them under his pillow and, most frequent of all, to ejaculate inside them. 'Spend your seed in these, you dirty beast' ordered a woman writing in purple ink on scented notepaper. 'And send them back to me at the above address.'

— For boiling, Annie. Definitely for boiling. I shall get Charlie to return them in person.

— Are you losing your wits, Mr Rudolf? What can you be thinking of?

— I am curious to discover what kind of floozy or hussy or foul-minded slut uses such Biblical language. Charlie will find out for me.

The 'offending objects' were duly boiled, and Charlie

instructed to inform their owner that Mr Rudolf Peterson was a firm believer in the adage —

— Be sure you say 'adage', Charlie. Adage, yes?

— Adage, Mr Rudolf. You are a firm believer in the adage —

— Excellent. Mr Rudolf Peterson is a firm believer in the adage that cleanliness is next to godliness. Study her reaction and report back to me.

My uncle was impatient all afternoon for Charlie's report.

— I wonder if she has lured him into her Biblical lair.

Charlie was thoughtful to the point of despondency when he returned to Nightingale Mansions.

— Demure's the word, Mr Rudolf. I handed her the box and told her Mrs Mackenzie had thoroughly boiled the thingumajigs inside and I passed on your message about the adage and that was when she blushed. She's demure and shy, Mr Rudolf. Not my type of girl in a million years. I just couldn't credit that she'd written you that letter. She's mousy, that's what she is, and ever so quiet-spoken.

My uncle, a connoisseur of the vagaries inherent in human nature, was satisfied with what Charlie had to tell him. He smiled sadly, and thanked his 'errand

boy' and promised that Mr Rudolf would never send
him on such an eccentric mission again.

— Leave the poor souls with their fantasies.

The routine of boiling and scrubbing continued.
Then, one day in 1946 Annie came into Uncle
Rudolf's music room at the house in Sussex, carrying
a brown paper parcel that was unexpectedly large and
as unexpectedly light.

— Dear God, she exclaimed upon opening it. I
wasn't wearing these things when I was married
to my lovely Gavin. They're bloomers, Mr Rudolf.
They're passion-killers. Look at them. (She held them
in front of her.) They start at the tummy and stop at
the knees.

— They will be the centrepiece, said my uncle,
those – what did you call them? – passion-killers.
Oh, I adore the idea of underwear killing passion.
It will appeal to Bogdan. I shall insist that he make
them the centrepiece.

And insist Uncle Rudolf did, though Bogdan Rangu
did not need much persuading when he mentioned
the idea of a collage to him. Bogdan was captivated by
the notion of collecting items of women's underwear
for the purpose of a surrealist painting and urged my
uncle to pass on everything his 'daring ladies' sent

him. This Uncle Rudolf duly did, despite Annie's protests that both he and that mad Mr Bogdan were making prize idiots of themselves. Some months later, the controversial painter had amassed enough material to start work – which he did, he declared, in a frenzy of excitement.

— Rudi, my dear friend, such serious fun I am having with these cast-offs.

The collage, which was entitled *Thoughts after Géricault, or The Raft of the Medusa Revisited*, was exhibited at a London gallery during the cruel winter of 1947. The title was, of course, one of Bogdan's jokes, a fact that didn't prevent several critics comparing his idiosyncratic assemblage to Géricault's masterpiece. The collage, which occupies an entire wall of the room where I am writing, is composed of a pair of red silk panties, cut in half; another pair, black, which a glum-looking priest is wearing as a hat; a brassiere supporting two empty milk bottles, and – in the centre, as Uncle Rudolf insisted – the voluminous bloomers, on which the words *Mort de passion* have been embroidered. In the background are photographs, variously torn or shredded, of film stars, birds, fish, disembodied arms, eyes, and legs, and a lavatory bowl, with the smiling face of Joseph Stalin peering out of it. Of all the works of art in my uncle's possession – the Gainsborough drawing of a falconer; the early Picasso painting of a young girl; the exquisite still life of a jug by Giorgio Morandi which the percipient collector bought for less than a hundred pounds in Rome in the 1950s – it was *Thoughts after Géricault* that attracted most comment and interest. Visitors to Nightingale Mansions would stare at it in bewilderment, shaking their heads in disbelief. Others, though, would laugh – and it was they who delighted my uncle, who would then reveal its esoteric origins.

— I could write a book, if I so desired, about the changing fashions in ladies' lingerie over the past thirty years. I was sent the first pair of drawers, as my darling Annie liked to call them, in Vienna in 1922, and I'm still getting them now that I'm retired. Not so many and not so often, God be thanked. I am glad Bogdan's agitated imagination was fired by those passion-killers.

When he introduced me to Bogdan Rangu, my uncle cautioned the artist not to speak the old words.

— Even your deplorable English will be beneficial to him. Our language belongs to my nephew's past. He is Andrew, remember – not Andrei.

— I shall try to endeavour to not forget, said Bogdan, winking at me. That is my solemn vow.

It was Bogdan's mischievous habit to assume facial expressions that suited whatever he was saying. A word like 'solemn' or 'serious' was accompanied by a look of quite absurd gravity, and when he said 'Don't be silly', which he did often, he would grin quickly and maniacally. The phrase was in direct contradiction to his espoused philosophy, which was founded on silliness. His 'Don't be silly' was the cue for laughter, an admonition to be ignored or denied. It meant, in reality, 'Be as silly as you can.' Hearing it now, in my mind, I feel suffused by such deep affection for his bravely comic spirit that I am on the verge of weeping. And, having written that last sentence, I hear 'Don't be silly' with renewed force, and I turn round and find myself looking at *Thoughts after Géricault* for the thousandth time and realizing that Stalin, smiling his murderer's smile, has been placed where he belongs – in shit; in, and with, perpetual shit. My tears remain in their ducts, as if at Bogdan's command.

— I am an exile by choice, not necessity, he once remarked to me, in French. I left when the life was good for fools and charlatans. I needed to transport my delight in everything ridiculous to a country where I would have to fight to see it appreciated. I chose sensible England, and I am still fighting. The Bucharest of my youth was so decadent and yet so provincial that I had to escape. I could have joined my friends and fellow artists in Paris, but that would have been an easy route to have taken. I thrive on hostility, Andrei – I am sorry, Andrew – and contempt, and I am richly supplied with both in London. Even Rudi considers me a little bit mad. And perhaps I am. Who am I to know?

It occurs to me, now, that Uncle Rudolf's sense of the sheer absurdity of human existence was as keen and refined as Bogdan Rangu's. That very sense, however, fuelled the discontent of his later years, whereas for Bogdan it provided a spur to creativity. I suppose I was honoured to witness the ritual of the parcels, because when I mentioned it to the boys I befriended at school they were shocked and surprised and, in one case, disgusted by what I had to tell them. I was being granted a glimpse of a world in which otherwise respectable women, driven by lust at my uncle's handsomeness, threw caution to the winds and made themselves unrespectable, if only for a moment. My incautious uncle saw no harm in my being educated in the often sad follies of humanity. And sometimes I understood that those winds were there for the purpose of having caution thrown at them, and sometimes – not being an artist – I didn't.

I had a wife once, and I have a son, to whom I was introduced when he was six and speaking with an American accent. I had seen and held him as a newborn baby. I had watched him in his cot, and woken in the night to cradle him back to sleep, and bathed him fondly, but then his mother took him away, without warning, leaving behind the briefest of notes to account for her sudden, unanticipated departure. It revealed to her gauche husband that she was in love with another man, and that she would raise William with his help. The note was unsigned.

Mary died long ago, of cancer, and her lover, who was forty years older, survived into senility. After his step-father's protracted death, William came to London to talk to the man he doesn't call Dad or Daddy or even Father. We found we wanted to be Andrew and Billy, as befits friends. It seemed natural not to address each other in terms of the roles we weren't allowed to play during his childhood and adolescence, when I was busy caring for his great-uncle, whose money – the hated Vienna money – he will inherit.

— Mummy never loved you, Andrew, Billy said late in the evening of our reunion. She was attracted to you, that was all.

— That was enough for both of us, at the time. We made an attractive couple. We had the charmed look about us, Billy.

— She hadn't the courage to tell anyone the man she loved was already old.

Neither had I, I didn't say. I was unaware, while I was married to Mary and beyond, of the true nature of my affections. I had no need of courage, then – my love for Uncle Rudolf being that of a devoted hero-worshipping nephew; my love for him being founded on evident gratitude for his rescuing me from a future that wasn't a future worth living. Courageousness was not to be considered or contemplated. That kind of courageousness was completely out of the question.

— Did Mummy tell you any of this, Andrew?

— She told me nothing.

— She was too frightened. Running off to America with him was her only option.

— She might have done it more tactfully, more politely. I was shaken. I was hurt. At the time.

— Mummy was guided by her feelings.

— Yes, Mummy was, and gained her freedom in the process.

— By all accounts, she and Joshua were happy together.

— Yes, they were. He was Josh to us. Josh was more down-to-earth, which he was, than Joshua.

— They caused quite a scandal, I told Billy, emphasizing 'at the time' yet again. Their names and photographs were in every gossip column. I was cast as the bravely smiling deserted husband, who only months before had led his beautiful young bride to the altar, and she was the gold-digging adulteress who had brought disgrace on her family and English society. Joshua was depicted as a wealthy child-snatcher, using his money to ensnare the gullible Mrs Peters into becoming his slave. On my uncle's advice, I remained silent throughout, even though it meant I incurred your grandfather's wrath as well as his lasting contempt. It was he who announced to the press that he would follow his daughter to the furthest flung parts of the world and bring her back to her home and her senses, and it was he who promised to horsewhip the devious Joshua Harris to within an inch of his dirty old man's life. As it was, he lost Uncle Rudolf's friendship and never left the country. Billy, I was, in truth, bewildered. My main anxiety was for you. I wanted news of you, and she never sent any, not a scrap, for two whole years.

— I'm sorry, Andrew. It's feeble, I know, but I'm sorry, very sorry.

I had not been granted the opportunity to be even an inadequate father, as we both acknowledged, with not a little irony.

It was then that Andrew and Billy shared a warm embrace, and then that their friendship was sealed.

— I am taking you to France, said my uncle. I intend to borrow you from your unmusical fiancée for at least ten days. You will find the excursion rewarding, I guarantee.

Was there a purpose to the trip, I asked, and was my presence necessary?

— Yes to the first question, and yes to the second. I still have a purpose to fulfil, and that purpose involves you.

— Are we going to Paris?

— Yes, we're starting out from there.

— I'm not sure that I ought to go. I'm not sure I can bear to be in Paris.

— I will be with you. You will be safe. Don't worry.

On the eleventh of September, 1950, I stood beside Uncle Rudolf and looked down on Paris from the top of the Eiffel Tower.

— I was a few months younger than you are now when I was here before. Oh, Andrew, I had such confidence. I really believed what my teacher in Botoşani had told me – that my voice was a gift from God. When you have God as your benefactor, my darling, you don't have any doubts. That's the Seine, he said, in a softer tone. That's the Seine, of course.

It was a fine autumnal day, a day for walking, and as we traversed the Rue des Deux Ponts the chill I felt after reading my father's letter swept over me once again. I was in its grip, and had to come to an involuntary halt. I shivered, like one in a fever.

— Do you want to go on?

I couldn't, at that moment, answer my uncle's question, because my tongue seemed incapable of moving.

— It isn't far, he murmured, taking my hand in his.

My cold, shaking hand in his steady, warm one. It isn't very far from here.

He led me, step by halting step, towards the Pont Marie, from which my father, his pockets weighted with stones, had hurled himself in the early morning of the twenty-seventh of February, 1937.

I stared at the calm water and tried to picture Tată – in his clerk's suit, the suit he wore on the train, the suit he was wearing as he waved me goodbye on the platform at the Gare du Nord, the suit he would leap to his death in – hesitating, perhaps, on this selfsame bridge; thinking, perhaps, of his son Andrei, who was only seven, and then not hesitating and not thinking, because to hesitate and to think of Andrei might give him a reason for living, and that was something he didn't want. I tried to picture him, smoking a cigarette, waiting for people to pass. But all I could see of him was on the platform, his sad face soon obscured by the steam from the engine.

— *La revedere*.

On the Pont Marie, staring in vain at the calm water that had closed over him, I mourned my father with resentful tears. I cursed him from the depths of my heart for not hesitating. The well-dressed Andrew Peters that I was cursed Roman Petrescu in his dull, frayed clerk's suit for not thinking of his only begotten son. And then I remembered that my mother had another's life inside her, and I begged and begged his forgiveness, in the old words he understood, without speaking.

I heard my uncle mumbling a prayer, and saw him make the sign of the cross.

I touched my protector's arm, which was quickly about me.

— Let's go. Let's go and gorge ourselves with lovely food. Come along.

My head was aching the next morning and my mouth dry, because – with Uncle Rudolf's encouragement – I had drunk too much champagne. I had shared a bottle of Fleurie with him at dinner and consumed several glasses of Armagnac afterwards. I had slept a drunkard's sleep for the first, and not the last, time.

He smiled as I joined him for breakfast. There was burnt toast on the table. The surly waiter, initially surprised by his strange request, had finally succumbed to his easy charm and exquisite French.

— A gallon of water for you, you scamp. We're setting off in an hour.

I asked him where we were going, but he answered

that our destination was a secret and would remain so until we reached it.

— We are driving in the direction of Fontainebleau today. That much I can reveal.

It was a relief to have Paris behind us, to sit close to my protector, who was more protective than ever, as he drove the modest car he cherished along dusty country roads. He sang for me sometimes from *Die Schöne Müllerin*, which he had been practising constantly with the uncomplaining Ivan, the seldom Terrible. *Dein ist mein Hertz, dein ist mein Herz* – he was fifty, but he might have been a pining, love-sick boy, so youthfully and jauntily anguished was the sound he made. It could have been me singing, if I'd a voice, of my own adolescent passion – except that mine hadn't been an adolescent's passion. I was attracted to Mary, but not to the extent of singing about her. I think I understood, on that autumnal day of reddening leaves, that if I'd had a voice it would be expressing either the grief I felt for my mother and father or the delight I was experiencing in my protector's company. If only I'd had a voice.

We arrived in Fontainebleau at dusk, when it was too late to visit the palace. I slept soberly in the small hotel where, as ever, burnt toast was provided for breakfast. On the thirteenth of September we were in Troyes; on the fourteenth we lunched in Chaumont and spent the night in Langres, and on the fifteenth we crossed the Saône at Arc and drove through Gray on the other side, reaching Besançon, our destination, in darkness. There was a music festival in progress in the city, and that evening we attended a reception in a grand hall where my uncle chatted to some of the artists who were taking part. I remember an elderly woman in a silver ballgown attaching herself to him, saying over and over that he was still the handsomest man in the world and that she had loved him half to death in Vienna.

— You are kind, Madame. He spoke with strained politeness.

— Oh, I am not kind in the least, Maestro. I saw your wonderful Danilo as often as I could. I was smitten. *Vraiment frappe.*

— Thank you, Madame.

— Oh, do not thank me, Maestro. It is you that must be thanked. You are a truly wicked man to retire so young.

— I am fifty, Madame. Fifty is not young.

— If you are young at heart it is, and you look young at heart. Fifty is nothing. You will, perhaps, be cajoled into singing for us while you are here, yes?

— I will, perhaps, be cajoled into singing for you while I am here, no. That is not the purpose of my visit. I have brought my nephew to Besançon for the sole purpose of opening his eyes and ears to the genius of Dinu Lipatti, the greatest pianist to come out of our beastly country. Goodnight to you, Madame.

Uncle Rudolf, seeing a musician he recognized, signalled to the man and led me across the hall to him. They talked only of Lipatti, and of the possibility that he would be too ill to play the following afternoon.

— I have brought Andrew to hear him. To watch him as well. I shall offer up a prayer on his behalf.

His praying woke me in the early hours. He had left his bed and was on his knees in front of the icon of St Nicholas, which he had placed on the dressing table.

— I packed him, Andrew. I thought he might be beneficial.

My uncle was on edge throughout the morning of the sixteenth of September. He was not alone in his anxiety, for everyone we met expressed concern about the pianist's health.

— I am being intolerably selfish, Andrew. I want him to perform today. I want something for both of us to remember.

We were to discover, when the recital was over, that Lipatti had willed himself into the Salle du Parlement de la Franche-Comté. In the late morning, after rehearsing, he suffered a feverish attack of such severity that his doctor was forced to tell him he would be incapable of playing. The organizers of the festival were informed by telephone of the decision. Then, on learning that every seat in the *salle* was occupied, Lipatti disobeyed his doctor's advice. It took him an eternity to dress; an eternity to walk to the waiting car that would bring him to the recital room. The audience was apprehensive, but strangely patient, for the hour the concert was due to begin had already passed. I can recall the intensity of feeling that seemed to possess everybody present. We were not to know, then, of the Calvary he had endured climbing the steps leading up to the Parliament House, nor that he had stood by the side of the platform clutching a hot-water bottle to warm his frozen hands.

The dark-suited Lipatti, more apparition than living man, came into view. We applauded as he made his slow progress to the piano. I heard Uncle Rudolf sigh.

It was no spectre who began to play Bach's First Partita. The apparition became on the instant radiantly animated. Were we aware of the perseverance, the superhuman fortitude, that propelled him that September afternoon? If we were, that would have been our sentimental illusion, since his undoubted fortitude was kept hidden by the pianist behind a necessary mask of civility. It was afterwards – after we had listened in coughless silence to the Mozart Sonata in A minor, two Schubert sonatas and a captivating string of Chopin waltzes – that we realized what an Olympian event we had been privileged to attend. We had not been watching a showman displaying his skills, nothing so predictable or commonplace. Lipatti was above display and superficial cleverness. He had played for us exactly what the composers had intended us to hear.

Uncle Rudolf was too moved to speak, and so was I. In the years to come, he would often refer to the miracle that had taken place in Besançon, for Lipatti never performed again in public, and died on the second of December that same year.

°   °   °

The woman in the market is shrieking the insult she first uttered sixty-four years ago. Her hatred persists. She will be cursing the Debt Collector's daughter until I die, though perhaps in my last moments she will show me some courtesy and be silent. Or perhaps, as seems likely, she won't.

The men who took my mother into the forest have no faces, no voices. The woman in the market is their spokesman, and it's her jeering face I see this morning as I saw it then, that far-off November.

— I have spoilt you long enough, said Uncle Rudolf, smiling. The time has come for you to be educated. I have found a teacher for you. I want you speaking English sooner rather than later.

— Yes, Uncle, I answered, in the new words.

— Mrs Watson will be here at nine tomorrow. Do not be frightened by her name, Andrew. She is Romanian.

What I chiefly remember of Marthe Watson is her hair. It must have been a human colour in the past – black, I suspect, or brunette – but now it was purple. I learned, eventually, that she dyed it regularly with henna.

— Do not stare at me in that rude manner, Andrew. You must always show respect to a lady.

— Yes, Mrs Watson.

— Say it and mean it. The future tense of the verb 'to have', if you would be so kind.

— I will have —

— Shall. Shall is correct.

— I shall have, Mrs Watson.

— Carry on.

I carried on, and faltered, and stammered, and within a month my vocabulary had increased considerably under my purple-haired teacher's strict tutelage.

— I forbid you to speak another word of Romanian, Andrew.

— Yes, Mrs Watson.

— Say something other than 'Yes, Mrs Watson', if you would be so kind. Give me an answer. In sentences.

— I promise not to speak one more word of Romanian. I promise to only speak English.

— 'English only'. You will keep that promise, Andrew.

As she was leaving that day, she spoke to my uncle in the language I was newly forbidden to speak in her presence. She despaired of what was happening in their country, she told him, and he agreed with her. He had been unhappy from the moment Carol the Second had ascended the throne.

The order established by Ferdinand and his brilliant wife Queen Marie had been dissipated. The alliance with Britain and civilized Europe was now in tatters. Romania was in spiritual and political ruins.

— *Evrei*, said Marthe Watson. They are the cause. They poison the world with their greed. They have poisoned Romania.

My uncle, reaching down to kiss me, whispered:

— Go to the kitchen, my darling, and have your tea. Annie is ready for you.

There was no purple hair to distract me the next morning. Marthe Watson's teaching had been successful, Uncle Rudolf couldn't deny, but she had opinions he had no wish for me to overhear. I would understand when I was older. There were too many people, not all of them Romanian, with opinions like hers.

— I will find you another teacher. You are an excellent student. I am proud of you.

My second tutor, Victor Collingham, had a bushy moustache which was constantly moist with saliva.

Victor was in the strange habit (to me) of chortling
to himself. Yes, chortling – a word unknown to me
then – is what he did. He never said anything funny
or silly – as Charlie and Teddy would, to make me
laugh – but he chortled even so. His other, stranger
habit was to refer to Mrs Collingham as *ma femme*.
'According to *ma femme*' he would begin, or 'As *ma
femme* is fond of saying' – scarcely a lesson would
pass without the thoughts of his *femme* being related
to me, his increasingly confused pupil.

— Mr Collingham, could you teach me a little
French?

— French? No, no. Definitely not. He chortled.

— Just a little.

— No, not even that much, Andrew. I don't speak
any French. A smidgen, and that's my limit. As *ma
femme* would no doubt observe: Victor Collingham,
you are not a linguist.

The chortler taught me to write thank-you letters
to those who had been kind to me and very short
short stories about the daily routine at Nightingale
Mansions. He marked passages in books – novels
or works of history – for me to read aloud. When I
stumbled over a difficult word, he gave me a chortling
explanation of its meaning. My brain was adrift with

nouns, verbs, clauses, adjectives and adverbs, but I
was determined to succeed for my uncle's sake and
to ensure he retained his pride in my excellence as
a pupil.

— *Ma femme* isn't best pleased I've been called
up for military service. She was under the mistaken
impression that I'm too old. I'm not, Andrew. I am
a decidedly elderly thirty-seven.

Victor Collingham said goodbye on the sixth of
April, 1940. His departure, with a chortle louder
and longer-lasting than all previous chortles, was the
subject of one of my very short short stories, which
Uncle Rudolf posted to him. To my dismay, there was
no reply. Perhaps – the word on which my life so often
seems to be founded – he was offended by what I, a
precocious ten-year-old, wrote about him. I did not,
could not, use words such as 'chortle' and 'saliva', but
my descriptions of his laugh and his moustache must
have offended him.

I know this with the enduring anguish of hindsight.

On my happiest days, in those first years in England,
I realized that I belonged to, and was the centre of,
an unusual family. I had no mother and father –

according to my uncle, they were lost or in hiding somewhere, but I did have a solicitous uncle (the word 'solicitous' is especially applicable); I had the doting Annie, who baked me cakes when I was well and nursed me with delicious soups and broths when I was sickly; and there was Teddy Grubb, with his card tricks that mystified a gullible boy and still mystify his fond remembrancer, and Charlie the chauffeur, whose Cockney accent he encouraged and dared me to mimic as he drove me through the city streets and down the narrow country lanes that led to Uncle Rudolf's Sussex home.

The wakeful Andrew Peters thrived in their company. They were united in a conspiracy to keep the poor little exile happy, and their every plan was successful. What a charmed decade or so that was – the more charmed when I recall the wartime blackout, with Annie making sure that not even the faintest chink of light could be seen through the windows, and the German bombs that seemed to be coming nearer and nearer with each new raid. It was charmed, too, despite my brief separation from Uncle Rudolf – the most degrading week of his entire life, he would tell me later – for by then I was in the relative safety of the countryside and free to play in the garden and roam in the surrounding fields. (He made fun of the white hairs that had suddenly sprouted on his temples, saying they were the inevitable consequences of growing old. He was forty-three.) My life at the grammar school was charmed as well, though I was terrified of being hit by a cricket ball in that most incomprehensible of games, with its terminology that sounded, and sounds, sublimely ridiculous. I learned English poems by heart, and acted as Florizel in a truncated version of *The Winter's Tale*, my brown-skinned Perdita a boy named Peter Long, and passed all my exams with 'flying colours'. I excelled in English, French and History and was never less than my uncle's pride. When my classmates asked where my parents were I repeated that they were lost or in hiding, and said I was unhappy that they did not know of my progress.

Charlie was the first conspirator to leave us. Maurice's imprisonment and despairing death – 'He wasted away, as if of his own accord' – caused him to suffer, and not endure, a grief he thought could be assuaged with gin, which he drank neat, at all hours. Uncle Rudolf was powerless to help or save him. He disappeared one day in the spring of 1949, leaving the car keys in an envelope with the message 'Goodbye and thank you very much, Mr Rudolf.' Nothing more. My uncle contacted his acquaintances, and even visited Maurice's mother; he telephoned every London hospital and gave the police Charlie's photograph, but there was no trace of him.

— He's vanished, Andrew. Off the face of the earth.

When it became a certainty that Charlie would never return, my uncle sold the Rolls-Royce in which I had been driven like a prince, and bought himself a small car that befitted, he said, his late-flowering modesty.

— I am not the singer I was. I am not like him any more.

Then Annie went, reluctantly, to nurse her ailing younger brother in Glasgow.

— He's blood, Mr Rudolf. You have to be loyal to blood. You can't turn a blind eye to it.

There was just Teddy left. In June 1950, he collapsed with a stroke at the racecourse when the horse he had bet on fell at the last hurdle. He had appropriated a thousand pounds of my uncle's money. The trusted, dutiful Teddy, who had entered every penny of Mr Rudolf's earnings in the ledgers he kept so scrupulously for fifteen years, was in serious debt, we learned, as the result of his infatuation for a younger woman with extravagant tastes.

Teddy only partially recovered. His speech, when he regained it, was slurred and difficult to comprehend. He was not to leave the nursing home my uncle paid for him to recuperate in. Nothing was seen or heard of the woman, whoever she was.

I picture Uncle Rudolf sitting at Teddy's bedside, gently stroking the hand that had, in his own shamed words, 'dipped into the till'.

— He would have paid the money back, and I would never have known it had gone missing. That wretched horse. That useless fool of a jockey.

— I had the proper kind of ambition once, before I was lured to Vienna by Hans Schenk. God curse him.

Herr Schenk was the villain in the story of my uncle's life, the original cause of the dismay that blighted his last years. I listened, and doubted Schenk's villainy. The Rudi Petrescu he was dazzled by in Nice was twenty and darkly handsome, as a photograph of him in costume testifies. His angelic voice apart, he was possessed of the looks and the sturdy physique that suited perfectly the irresistible heroes of operetta – those gypsies; those princes; those gypsy princes;

those troubadors, vagabonds and brigands; those detested Cossacks and Hussars.

Uncle Rudolf would like to tell how the astute entrepreneur had pushed his way into the men's dressing room after the performance, and ignored the Don Giovanni and the Leporello and announced to the startled Rudi Petrescu that a contract to sing in Vienna was his for the accepting. It was Schenk's considered plan to get him cast in cameos to begin with – two or three at most – before his remarkable gifts secured him the leading roles he was born to assume. Those leading roles were not to be the ones he and Jean de Reszke had envisaged.

Schenk became Rudi Petrescu's manager, working tirelessly on his behalf, persuading sceptical impresarios to let him audition. Within three years, the newly-named Rudolf Peterson was taking on important parts – Alfred in *Die Fledermaus*, and then, most famously, Danilo in *The Merry Widow*. He was rich, he was fêted, and he had several affairs, the only one of any consequence being with Hilde Bernhard, whom I met at his funeral.

— The wisest decision I ever made in my otherwise foolish life was not to marry your uncle. Andrew dear, marriage with Rudi would have been like a play by Strindberg. A minuet, if not a dance, of death. You tell me he was melancholic, but he was melancholic at the height of his career, when he and I were passionately in love. Even then there was something gnawing at him he couldn't talk about. This is exceptional champagne.

— It was his favourite. *La grande Dame*. It was one of his few consolations.

— Ah, Rudi. Always in need of consoling.

I thought I knew what had been gnawing at him. I had written evidence, in the form of two letters, both dating from the 1920s. I showed them to Hilde Auersberger, as she now was, that evening, after the other mourning guests had gone.

(The first is from Jean de Reszke. He wrote to M. Petrescu in 1924, some months before his death, to this effect. I have translated it from the French):

My dear young friend and pupil.
Minia, Louis, Amherst and I read news of your success almost daily. We send you our congratulations and warm greetings. I predicted fame for you, in my silent fashion, and now you have found it.

Permit me to offer you some words of advice. As your teacher, I believe I am qualified so to do. In my long years in opera – both as a baritone and then (wonderful discovery) as a tenor – I had occasion to sing music that was mediocre or worse. Who now remembers M. Bemberg's Elaine, in which I played Lancelot? I remember and shudder. It is time you ordered the persuasive Herr Schenk to arrange for you to number Messieurs Verdi, Bizet, Mozart and Wagner among your musical acquaintances. You should be Radames, Don José, Don Ottavio, Lohengrin and, one day perhaps, Tristan himself. You should not confine yourself to operetta. You have wings to be stretched, and the talented Herr Johann Strauss and the whimsical Lehar will not stretch them for you. Think of your art, my diligent pupil, and of your artistry. I demand that you think of them now that you are rich and famous.

The voluble Koko has just screeched salutations.

I embrace you paternally, Jean de Reszke.

P.S. Try not to be a STUPID tenor. With a vacant space in his head.

The letter from Georges Enesco, dated 30 May, 1929, is in the old words, which I translated for Hilde's benefit. It runs as follows:

Dear Rudi Petrescu or Rudolf Peterson – You are embarked on a course that I must tell you I find regrettable. When I heard you singing Mozart at the Conservatoire ten years ago I had hopes of your becoming one of those great artists who put music before such transient matters as fame. Those hopes are being dashed every time you appear in yet another piece of froth. This is a sadness for me and for our country. I want you to know my feelings and to give them serious consideration. You are still young. I entreat you to change direction. Your friend in music. G.E.

— He said nothing of these to me, Andrew. Or, I suspect, to anyone else. He kept them his very close secret.

— And from me, too. I found them only yesterday. I wonder why he kept them – as reminders, perhaps, of what he might have been – and if he ever replied. I think he must have answered those letters, because de Reszke and Enesco were his heroes and he believed in courtesy. He might have promised to change his ways. And then he couldn't. He said to me once, when he was very unhappy, that he would have had a better life if he had been born plain, or even ugly. Then his voice, and his voice alone, would have justified his existence.

I did not mention Uncle Rudolf's love for my mother to the sprightly Hilde, who looked much younger than seventy-four, but I did tell her about the humiliation of his last public recital, for which he had prepared so long and so thoroughly with Ivan Morris.

I remembered that he came on to the platform and scanned – I think that's the accurate word – the audience. He registered that it was largely composed of middle-aged and elderly women – the same women who had flocked to see him in *Magyar Maytime* and the other operettas he despised. He stared at his applauding fans as if they were his enemy, which – in a way – they were. He was about to become the boyish miller who is helplessly in love with the boss's daughter – *die schöne Müllerin*. His face showed only contempt. Then he shook his head, smiled, and signalled to Ivan he was ready to begin. He sounded nervous to start with, but he did manage to capture the youthful ardour in those first ravishing songs. Then, in the ninth song, the one that tells of the bright blue flowers growing by the stream that remind him of his sweetheart's eyes, his voice cracked on *'Fensterlein'* (her window), and he gasped for air and forgot the rest of the words while Ivan played gamely on. 'Enough,' he said loudly. 'Your money will be refunded. Goodnight.' He walked out of the concert hall and continued walking for several hours. When I saw him next, it was two in the morning.

— When we were together – in Budapest and Paris, as well as in Vienna – he gave no indication that his melancholy moods had anything to do with the shows we were performing. No indication at all.

— He claimed that Hans Schenk lured him away from the music he ought to have sung. He called him a villain.

— A villain, Hans? No, no – he was a shrewd businessman, who made your uncle very rich. Rudi never complained when Hans presented him with a large cheque. It seems from what you are saying that he should have had the courage to follow de Reszke's advice. He didn't. He must have been afraid. He sang Danilo with such happy confidence, Andrew. He relished every note. No wonder the public adored him. Have you any more of that champagne? Let's toast the happiness he brought into the world.

— Let's.

— What on earth is that on the wall? How could I have missed it? Am I really that drunk?

— No. It's a collage. *Thoughts after Géricault, or The Raft of the Medusa Revisited*, to give it its full title. There's a story behind it.

— I'm sure there is.

I related the story, in the meticulous, and often diverse, detail that comes with tipsiness, but had to stop to accommodate Hilde's tearful laughter.

— Prostitutes would have exercised more decorum. Ladies, indeed.

I was back in the everlasting market this morning, but this time the woman wasn't there. Uncle Rudolf, surprisingly, was. He was waiting to greet me, dressed in that same astrakhan coat he wore in February 1937, on the platform at Victoria Station.

— Welcome home, he said.

What age was I? Was I seven again? I could neither see nor hear myself.

— You have your mother's beauty.

He had said this to me, in English, in 1946, after my one and only appearance on a stage. I had played Florizel that evening, as I reminded him when he commented on my beauty. The other boys in the makeshift dressing room blushed and giggled.

— I was Florizel, Uncle Rudolf. Not Perdita.

— I know you were, Andrew. It's your eyelashes, that's all. They are very like your mother's.

In the market, in his astrakhan coat, he beckoned Andrei to come to him.

— You have your mother's beauty, he told the nephew he never called Andrei, in the language he had rarely spoken to him.

I am tempted to destroy what I have written so far, and nearly did so today after my uncle, my dead uncle, had coaxed me to him, only to vanish. Perhaps I should have embarked on a biography of him as I once intended to – listing the relevant facts and dates, and keeping myself to myself. But that's a book I am unable to write, if only because my life – such as it is, what is left of it – is inextricably linked to his. I cannot be disinterested.

And that is why I have to go on, writing late into

the night, warding off as many dreams as I can, summoning my beloved ghosts to me. And now I catch myself laughing as I stop and think of this whole ludicrous enterprise. For who will read these pages? My contentedly married son, perhaps, whose unworldly wife may have to be spared my one truly shocking revelation, which I have yet to make, if I ever will.

— I was surprised they didn't take you in for questioning as well, Andrew. You were eleven, and that's a dangerous age. I'm sure they're employing eleven-year-old spies in our beastly country.

Why, I asked, had they – whoever they were – taken him in for questioning?

They, he said, were officials in the War Office, who had discovered – it was no secret – he was Romanian by birth. Romania was in league with Germany, ergo: a singer of operetta who had not been in Bucharest for almost a decade was bound to be under suspicion for something or other. He was a respected British citizen, what's more, which meant he was a likely traitor, traitors being masters of plausible disguise. He had to be guilty, and they – the two men and a ferocious woman in tweeds –

were intent on proving it. He was detained for the most degrading week of his entire life, locked in a room that only the most severely self-lacerating monk would have found congenial. And, yes, a spotlight was trained on him – but then, he was accustomed to the spotlight, having sung many a rousing call for liberty and justice in its inspiring glow. They questioned him when he was on the point of sleep, or desperate to go to the lavatory, or scared of confessing to a crime he was incapable of committing, in the interests of being left in peace. They were diligent. They were determined to have him admit he was in the pay of General Antonescu, the ruler of Romania, if not Adolf Hitler. And then, at the peak of his degradation, he had said to them:

— Look, the three of you, my brother's wife was dragged into the forest by three men whose ideology you are accusing me of espousing and supporting with money. My brother drowned himself in Paris, leaving me to raise his orphaned son. Am I that devious, that cunning? I seem to be in the thrall of two diabolical holy trinities.

— I was delighted with that unhappy conceit, my darling. It eased my pain, saying it. For one sarcastic moment, anyway. Yes, for that one sarcastic moment

– and it *was* nothing longer than a moment – I felt I had riled them as they were riling me. I was mistaken, of course. They resumed their questioning with a fresh sense of purpose. And when they let me go it was without apology. Why should they apologize for nearly succeeding in breaking me? They had been trained, and paid, to do exactly that. They shuffled up their papers and left me alone for an hour or so. Then a man I hadn't seen before came in and said the car was ready. I was untied from the chair. He waited for me to stand up. He placed a sheet over my head and guided me out of the room and the building but not out of the degrading experience. No one can ever do that. Sometimes when I'm lying in the bath I have this notion of a water that can cleanse the soul of all its torments, the way water cleanses the body. You pour some of it on the worst of your memories, drop by drop, and they vanish like a stain vanishes. They're eradicated.

I hear my uncle saying this, and remember how deeply he was scarred by those six days in the summer of 1941, when his precious conscience – as precious to him as the praise he had earned from Jean de Reszke – was not simply questioned but maligned and soiled. The two men and the tweeded woman could not have known with what sudden fierce disdain he had responded to Marthe Watson's remark about the *evrei* (I use the old word because it conjures up for me the venom with which she spoke it) and that the otherwise satisfactory teacher was dismissed on the instant. They scoffed at him when he referred to the once beloved, but now beastly, country he had abandoned, and did not believe his repeated claim to be a contented and responsible exile, as anxious as anyone to see Hitler and his vile henchmen destroyed. They reminded him that he had sung in German, and he reminded them that he had also sung in English and French. He refrained, absurdly, from adding Italian and Hungarian, sensing that his mentioning them might inspire the deadly trio to accusations of his being on the side of Fascism.

— There was one terrible day, Andrew, when I would have been happy to be that idiot Zoltan again, declaring to Zelda that his heart was hers and hoping, oh so fondly, that hers was his in return. Just think, my darling, how seriously distressed I must have been to have even considered such a prospect. I had reached the very lowest of all lowest ebbs. I couldn't have plunged any further.

Uncle Rudolf gave me a wan smile and then, as if

fully realizing the preposterousness of his admission, he laughed as I hadn't heard him laugh for months. Yet it was, in its intensity, I understood, the laughter of despair.

On one of those afternoons that stayed sunlit for my uncle – he had merited a *bien* – the master invited his brightest pupil to drink some wine and eat some biscuits. This was the rarest privilege. Rudi Petrescu, in his confusion, found that he couldn't reply. While he struggled for the one simple word of acceptance, Louis Vachet entered bearing a tray.

— Monsieur Petrescu has accepted my invitation, Louis.

The wine was an iced rosé, the biscuits orange wafers. Rudi had guessed that his teacher was in the mood to reminisce, and – prompted by Louis Vachet – that is what he did, for far too short a time. What made the occasion memorable for the gawping student was not the fact that de Reszke and his brother had performed at Windsor Castle in private audience with Queen Victoria, but rather the master's way of reliving the great roles he had blessed with his genius. He spoke, that afternoon, of Otello, a part he had accepted with reluctance, since he was

ill when he was first offered it, and although he loved
Verdi's music it was against his temperament to play
a murderer.

— A very silly reason, Monsieur Petrescu. I think
you will agree that, on this disturbed planet of ours,
some murderers are nobler than others. The misguided Otello is one of them.

De Reszke had been influenced in his conception
by the actor Tommaso Salvini, whom he had seen in
Shakespeare's tragedy.

— It is instructive to study actors. They are often
more musical than singers. If they do not respect the
language, they are booed and hissed off the stage.
They have no beautiful noises to hide behind.

De Reszke got up from his chair, stubbed out his
cigar and picked up a cushion. He looked down at the
carpet, to which he pointed:

— That is my Desdemona. Is she breathing? I have
robbed her of life with this pillow. Or have I? Let me
look closer.

He was speaking, as always, in French, but now –
now that he was Otello – he was singing and speaking,
the two conjoined, in Italian:

. . . e stanca, e muta, e bella

— Oh, Andrew, his voice was eerie, full of horror and wonder. Horror at what he, Otello, had done, and wonder at the thought of her spirit floating away from him. He invested so much feeling in those nine syllables – 'e stanca, e muta, e bella'. No, I can't do it. I can't match him. Why should I pretend to? And this carpet is no Desdemona, either.

I was serenaded to sleep by my newly-met uncle on the night of 23 February, 1937, with one of the folk songs Brahms wrote for the children of Clara Schumann, the woman who could not reciprocate the idolatrous love he felt for her. It is called 'The Guardian Angel', though I did not know it then. I can't say that my ears were immediately ravished – that ravishment was to happen at Christmas, when Uncle Rudolf summoned up a whole host of angels, wafting Jephtha's daughter, Iphis, to the skies – but they were pleased enough to want him to sing to me again. And, with time, I came to understand that the music he sang and played to me on the piano, or made me listen to on his gramophone, was not the music with which he was associated by his admirers. That music, tuneful as it was, and insidiously easy to remember – as he once observed scathingly – had to be cast aside, and for reasons that weren't entirely musical. One of those reasons, certainly the most pitiful, was the fate of my parents, which I would not learn about until I was eighteen, on the evening of the two medicinal brandies. He came to believe that operetta, frivolous as it was, grew out of the culture that killed them, and that it was his duty to protect me from it. And when he bade farewell to the 'sinister nonsense' in December 1945, it was in the cause of the survivors of millions of Debt Collector's daughters and sons who had perished. He sang 'Goodnight, Vienna' with a contempt that was blissful to him, for it was in that city of cream cakes and Nazis that he had made the reputation he scorned. There would be no more Cossacks, no more Hussars, no more roguish brigands and gypsies unaware of the royal blood in their youthful veins. He was the same age as the century, and he wanted no more of operetta. He was greeted with sustained cheering, and he took a dozen bows as the result of that contemptuous encore, but when we were back in Nightingale Mansions he said:

— That was the best enema ever, my darling. I've cleared the shit out of my system. I feel lighter already.

I think, if I am honest, that I was disappointed by his decision to retire. I had loved the hours in his dressing room or by the side of the stage when his lucky mascot brought him the ill luck he craved. Young as I was, I sensed that he could not renew his career in serious opera, judging by the conversations I overheard, or to which I was party, with his agent or with the managers of houses in both London and Paris. He was now too old to take on Ferrando and Don Ottavio and he lacked the experience to tackle the weightier roles in the tenor repertoire. He pleaded for an opportunity to prove himself. He had been the prize pupil of Jean de Reszke; and Georges Enesco, who was still alive, would vouch for the true nature of his talent, if contacted. But the master had died in 1925, and Enesco had heard him sing in the Bucharest Conservatoire as long ago as 1918. The dates told his sad story. They were like insurmountable boulders on his path.

Our trip to Besançon – our pilgrimage, rather, for such it turned out to be – was Uncle Rudolf's most astute gift to his darling nephew, coming so soon as it did upon the grief his revelations had released. It was his sweet purpose to have me sit for the hour or so of Lipatti's recital and be educated in the finer aspects of the human spirit. It was a more than musical offering I received that September afternoon – it was a lesson in self-abnegation and self-transcendence. My uncle and I were speechless for hours afterwards, his only words being those to a barman when he ordered a bottle of claret.

We were on the point of leaving the following morning when we noticed Lipatti signing programmes for a small group of people, some of them musicians. My uncle joined the group, pulling me along with him. I was embarrassed to be in such a presence, but the grip on my wrist was firm.

— I do not require your autograph, my uncle said in French. I want to thank you, that is all. My nephew wishes to thank you also.

— Thank you very much, I said, reddening as he took my hand and shook it.

— Thank you both for thanking me. You are gracious.

I met my future wife, my wife of a year and a bit, when she came to play with me in the garden behind my uncle's country house. We were twelve years old. Three years later, we were still friendly, though we didn't indulge in those games of bodily exploration that children who are mutually attracted are supposed to indulge in. We kept our physical distance.

It was Uncle Rudolf whose arms she rushed into, whose face she covered with kisses. These shows of affection did not surprise me. It was safe for a girl of her age to flirt with a man in his forties – safer by far, it was assumed, than if she had flirted with me. I can't remember, now, what we had in common, if anything. Oh yes, I recall that, under my uncle's expert tuition, we became adept at tennis. We once played mixed doubles against her parents, whom we beat in straight sets. That day, at least, we were as one. We allowed ourselves a winners' embrace.

I am being cynical. We were pleasantly disposed to one another. We were constantly reminded of our attractiveness, to the extent that we began to accept that it was our destiny, nothing less, to marry. Even my uncle, who deplored Mary's complete lack of interest in music, shared the general view in the Sussex society we moved in that it would be a shame if such an attractive couple didn't tie the marriage knot. Mary must have been conscious of the fact that she was suppressing her true feelings, especially when the American financier, Joshua Harris, came to stay with her family in the summer of 1950. The innocents were engaged by then. I now remember that Mary wasn't remotely disconcerted or upset when Uncle Rudolf requested that he 'borrow' me for a week's trip to France in September.

— I can spare him for a week, Mr Rudolf. After all, I shall be spending a lifetime with him.

Joshua Harris returned to England the following June, and sat at the back of the village church to watch us being married. At the wedding feast, for which my uncle supplied the champagne, Mary's father amused the guests when, in the course of his speech, looking at the bride and groom, he quipped:

— You two are rivals in prettiness. I trust you know which one of you is which.

Prophetic words, indeed. The joke induced both laughter and applause. I was accustomed to having my eyelashes envied by women and commented on by men, but only Uncle Rudolf had said I was beautiful. 'Prettiness' was new to me. 'They make a pretty couple' became the alternative to 'They make a handsome couple' after Colonel Spragge's address.

We took our honeymoon in Rome, where we were surprised and delighted to see farmers selling their livestock in Piazza di Spagna. The first thing we heard as we made for the Spanish Steps was the bleating of sheep. We laughed, imagining such a spectacle in Trafalgar Square or Piccadilly Circus. I was alone when I visited the house in which Keats died, Mary considering my wish to pay homage to my favourite poet 'morbid'. We strolled happily through the ruins of the Forum, but Mary had no desire to accompany me to the Colosseum. The thought of gladiators slaughtering, or being slaughtered by, wild beasts repelled her. This future lover of a man on the verge of old age had no interest in, or curiosity about, human history.

My uncle had arranged for us to be put up in the Hotel Excelsior, and it was there that Billy was conceived, in the very lap of luxury. Mary was patient with her fumbling, sexually immature husband, whom she astonished with her skilfulness in rendering what was flaccid halfway forceful. On the third day, I rose again, thanks to her exertions.

We lived in London, in a service flat in Westminster, not far from the Catholic cathedral. It was there that Mary had her clandestine meetings with the adoring Joshua while I was working as my uncle's secretary and bookkeeper in Nightingale Mansions. They were, I was to be told by Billy, particularly fond of evensong on Wednesday afternoons, when they held hands to the accompaniment of Palestrina or William Byrd, neither of whom Mary would have appreciated. Their romance flowered to that unheard music. They could pretend, as they joined the congregation, they were already united.

How old was Billy when she deserted me? Three months? Four? Somewhere between, I suppose, since she absented herself from our jogtrotting marriage in mid-July 1952. I think I was offended more than hurt, for I quickly realized it was my son I missed in the days following her departure. I came to realize, too, during the profound and menacing silence she maintained for two years or more, that it was Billy I wanted to hold and kiss, not Mary. She could remain wherever she was, I decided. It was his safety, his welfare, that preoccupied me through many months of anguished speculation.

Colonel Spragge's splenetic outbursts against the scheming philanderer with one foot in the grave who had stolen his daughter from under the family's nose were recorded verbatim in the newspapers. He would horsewhip the bounder (delightful word) within an inch of his dirty old man's life. The 'bravely smiling' cuckold said nothing, as did Cicely Spragge, a taciturn adjunct to her voluble spouse, and as did Uncle Rudolf, who – being famous – was asked the most questions by the press.

The colonel called on my uncle at Nightingale Mansions. Their conversation – or, to be precise, Colonel Spragge's scarcely interrupted monologue – had hardly progressed beyond insults before he was shown the door and advised not to come back. From Mayfair he proceeded to Westminster. His persistent ringing of the doorbell alerted me to the undoubted fact that an argument was in the offing. Something much more unsettling was to occur.

— Come in, I said. May I fix you a drink?

— There's no drink strong enough to calm me down. No, you can't fix me a drink. What you can do for me is explain what kind of man it is who can lose his wife to a liver-spotted Yid who's older than her father.

— You are referring to me?

— Who else?

I was incapable of giving him an answer. He fumed, loudly.

— You couldn't satisfy her down there, is that it?

— I gave her a son.

— Wonder of wonders. Stop fluttering those pretty eyelashes and tell me the truth.

— What truth?

— The truth about your failure as a husband.

— She loves Mr Harris, or his money. She doesn't love me, that's clear.

— Why should she love a man who can't fulfil his natural duty?

I suggested, with great restraint, that he seek out Mr Harris, horsewhip him as threatened, bring his daughter to her senses as promised, and to leave me to take stock of my myriad inadequacies in private. I wondered, politely, why he was so obsessed with my eyelashes, which were nature's doing, not mine, and invited him to accept a calming drink.

— You speak the fancy English of a foreigner. Everything's foreign about you, including your disgusting prettiness. You don't even *look* like a man.

I wished him goodnight, and a safe and pleasant journey back to the country. I hoped he would have the courtesy to pay my respects to Mrs Spragge, whom I had been pleased to call my mother-in-law.

Here I am on a February morning, being lifted from

my bed by Tată, who is smiling down on me. It is dark outside. A candle is burning faintly in a corner of the room.

— Is Mamă home? I ask, as I had asked the day before, and the day before that.

— Not yet, my dear one. She will be home when you come back from your wonderful holiday with Uncle Rudi. I think you must call him Uncle Rudolf, now that he is a famous singer.

— I want to wait here for Mămică.

— I know you do. But your uncle has written to me saying that he really must see his one and only nephew, and he would be very unhappy, Andrei, very unhappy, if you did not go.

— Show me the funny picture again, Tată.

He takes from his pocket the photograph he will give the guard in Paris. I ask Tată if my uncle Rudi or Rudolf always has rings in his ears and a sword in his belt.

— No, no. He is playing a part, Andrei. On a stage. In a theatre. You will visit a theatre in London, I promise. That will be exciting for you.

— Are you coming to London, Tată? I ask, hoping that his answer will be different from the one I heard yesterday.

— I told you, Andrei. I have business in Paris. Important business, my sweet one. You will feel very grown-up, having a holiday without me.

— And Mamă.

— And Mamă, yes. And Mamă. My brother is a kind man, as I must have told you a hundred times. You will be safe with him.

— I am safe here, Tată.

— I can hear Mircea's horse. Listen. Clip clop, clip clop. You have five minutes to do what you need to do. And then we must wash and dress you and get you ready.

He lowers me to the floor.

— Be quick, he says. Be as fast as you can. Hurry, hurry, lazybones. We have a train to catch, remember.

We are in the hallway. A thought comes to me, which I say out loud.

— Mamă has left her icon behind, Tată. She took it with her when she went away last time.

— Did she?

— Yes, Tată. She has to pray to the Virgin every day. You know she has to.

He is lost for words, or lies. He tells me to hurry or we shall be late and then I will miss my holiday with Uncle Rudolf. And what a pity that would be.

— Mamă's faith will come to her aid, Andrei.

My mother's helpful faith. My father's business in Paris. The beginning of the end of the old words.

In 1955, my uncle left Nightingale Mansions and sold his Elizabethan manor. He was through, he said, with the grand way of life. Now that it was certain that he would never sing in public again, he wanted to live modestly, anonymously. He moved, and I moved with him, to a house in west London, with a view of the Thames.

— Not quite the Mediterranean, but it will do as second best.

Even though he had retired, there was enough work to occupy his secretary and bookkeeper. There were royalty statements from the record company that had once had him under exclusive contract; fan letters to answer and have him, reluctantly, sign; requests to make appearances on radio and television light entertainment programmes which had to be refused without his ever knowing about them; journalists and impresarios to keep at bay. These last were especially difficult to fend off, because they were the most insistent in their demands to interest Mr Peterson in touring revivals of *The Gypsy Baron* and *The Desert Song*.

Uncle Rudolf came into my office while I was explaining to a brash theatrical manager, in tones of willed calmness, that the great star of operetta had chosen to become a recluse. Yes, I repeated, a recluse. Like a monk. He had cut himself off from his past and almost everything associated with it.

— Tell him, Andrew, that I am absorbed these days in the works of Béla Bartók.

And this was true. He was completely absorbed. Bartók's place in his musical re-education, as he called it, was paramount, for here was the one composer who sent him back in memory to a childhood of folk song and gypsy music in a country that had yet to turn bestial. He even recognized some of the tunes Bartók had picked up and notated on his travels through Hungary and Romania in 1916. He talked of the *tilincă*, a stringed instrument the shepherds played, and said the sound of Bartók reminded him of yet other sounds – of insects, birds, horses, cattle. This was the natural world he was born into and revelled in as a boy, along with Roman and their fellow scamps, before his life was taken over by, and with, the worst kind of artifice. While I sat at my desk upstairs, dealing with the remnants of his career, I would often stop and listen to him coming to somewhat uncertain grips with the complexities of *Mikrokosmos* on the grand piano below. On calmer days, he would be content with the early pieces such as the *Fourteen Bagatelles* or the *Three Burlesques* or, most poignant of all, the *Two Romanian Dances* of 1910, the year in which he first discovered that God had presented him with the voice of an angel.

If he wept, he said, I was not to attempt to comfort him. He had a handkerchief at the ready. Any tears he shed would be those of happy reminiscence. I was not to be alarmed or upset. I was to leave him with his thoughts.

How could I leave him to his thoughts when they so often impinged on my own? I was the contented prisoner of his melancholy, I realize now, and in no manner prepared to escape from it. The prison's alarm system would not, could not, go off. The guards and warders had been freed to take a permanent holiday.

I was the diligent Andrew by day, studying hard to impress his uncle and the teachers who afforded him special attention, but at night, invariably, I was the terrified Andrei, chasing after his uncatchable parents. The two seldom merged, but on one occasion, during a rehearsal of *The Winter's Tale* on the stage in the school hall, Andrew, unable to say the lines

> . . . When you do dance, I wish you
> A wave o' th' sea, that you might ever do
> Nothing but that; move still, still so,
> And own no other function . . .

without faltering over 'A wave o' th' sea', because of the missing 'f' and 'e', became, in a frustrated instant, the boy in the snow, blinded by whiteness. It was the old words he heard himself spluttering, to the amazement of his dusky Perdita and the concern of Mr Harper, who was producing the play.

— Drink some water, Peters. Take a deep breath and look at me. Trust me, but trust Shakespeare more. Give yourself the faintest 'e' as a present and the line is yours to command.

I was determined, on the evening of the performance, not to let Andrei into Bohemia, of which country, I, Florizel, was prince. I came to the line and spoke it quickly, almost unthinkingly, and the frightened child was banished. He reappeared briefly in the dressing room afterwards, when Uncle Rudolf said I had my mother's beauty, but that was an embarrassment the sharp-witted Andrew Peters made light of with skill. I had coped with the most difficult, the most complex, poetry in English, and I felt proud at having done so. Compared to my classmates and fellow actors, all of them aged sixteen, I was but a nine-year-old in the language. I had good reason, I told myself, for pride.

Uncle Rudolf had brought an actress to watch me as Florizel. I glowed from her compliments. Her name has gone, but I do recall that she had very long blonde hair and that she had once played Ophelia – her only excursion (I remember the word) into Shakespeare, she said. Charlie drove the three of us back to the manor. Annie, hearing the car crunch to a halt in the driveway, came out on to the steps to greet me. Although I was tall and confident (by day, at least) I was still her poor, lovely little boy – the goggle-eyed waif she had hugged almost to breathlessness on 23 February, 1937 – and that was how she addressed me as she took me into her arms to enquire how I had fared. It was the actress who gave the answer. In her opinion, I had fared wonderfully.

Annie had baked a special cake for me, with a layer of the marzipan I loved. There were sixteen candles to blow out.

— I've had my birthday already, Annie.

— This is to celebrate your arrival as a true English schoolboy, speaking Shakespeare like a native, Uncle Rudolf explained. This is more important than any birthday.

My triumph as a verse speaker (I blush to think what my acting was like) was toasted in champagne, of which I was allowed one glass, filled to the brim. I was sent off to bed with kisses, and remained Andrew Peters throughout the night and into the early morning hours, unable to sleep for joy.

Let me now write, with some sadness, of Annie, whose departure from the unusual family bewildered my uncle and mortified me. She had seemed immovable. Only death itself, the vanquisher of every constant, could take her from us, we assumed. She said she was reluctant to go, but blood was blood, and you had to be loyal to it. Her ailing brother needed her. He had no one else to care for him in the entire world.

— Bring him to London. I will pay for nurses to tend him.

— Bruce would never accept charity, Mr Rudolf. It's kind of you to offer. No, I shall have to shift my old bones up to Glasgow, though it breaks my heart to leave poor lovely Andrew behind.

We saw her off at Euston Station on a drizzly October morning. My uncle kept shaking his head in disbelief as we carried her bags into the first-class compartment in which he had reserved a seat for her. He urged her to change her mind at the eleventh hour and come back to Nightingale Mansions where she belonged. He pleaded with her. Look, he said, here's the ticket. Give me permission to tear it up and you'll make me very happy. And your poor, lovely, not-so-little Andrew, too.

— You will do no such thing, Mr Rudolf. Give me the ticket and be off with the pair of you, before I start to blub. I can't abide partings.

And so we left her, with me promising to write, and Annie demanding that I keep my promise, and Uncle Rudolf making a last attempt to dissuade her from going. She hugged me to her, and embraced my uncle. We were speechless and bereft in the taxi taking us back to the rooms in Nightingale

Mansions she had graced with her clucking kindli-
ness.

For it was Annie's way to express disapproval of
Mr Rudolf's alien habits by pretending to be what
she clearly wasn't – an archetypal Scottish prude,
the stern product of an unyielding Calvinism. Her
clucks and frowns were parodic in essence, as if she
were commenting ironically on the shocked reactions
of a genuine daughter of the kirk. She had much
to cluck about, given the number of affairs Uncle
Rudolf indulged in before and after I entered his
life. These had been related to me by the envious
and admiring Charlie. Annie had been widowed for
twenty years when she first took me in her crushing
arms. A framed photograph of her husband in the
uniform of a Highland regiment was always at her
bedside. She cleaned the glass every day, and kissed
his image every night. She was faithful unto eternity,
she said. Yet the token cluck and the studied frown
were all she exhibited to indicate that Mr Rudolf,
her employer and friend, was not like other steady,
reliable men – the kind who take marriage vows and
stick to them, for richer or poorer, in sickness and
in health. Annie was deeply fond of my uncle, whom
she once described as a 'scallywag'. There would have

been no scallywags to amuse and tease her if her
beloved Gavin had not been killed in the Battle of
the Somme. She smiled wistfully at the thought.

Whenever she talked about her brother Bruce, it
was not in flattering terms. She used a word I came
to love on her lips – 'wastrel'. Bruce was a wastrel,
a good-for-nothing, a scrounger. He was perpetually
short of money, due to his craving for strong drinks,
and had been ill with a catalogue of complaints, all
of which – she believed – were of his own inventing.
If she ever lost touch with Bruce (which, God help
her, was a blessing she deserved), she would be sure
to find him in one of two places – the saloon bar of
the Young Pretender or his doctor's waiting room.
The chances of his turning up, begging cap in hand,
at Nightingale Mansions were happily remote. From
the pub to the surgery, the surgery to the pub – that
was how he filled his days, the wastrel.

So it was a surprise to me, and to my uncle
– who knew more of Bruce's drunken misadven-
tures than I did – when Annie announced that
she was determined to be at her ailing brother's
side for what might be his final illness. As it was,
he outlived her by five years. We attended her
funeral, the cost of which was met by Uncle Rudolf,

although the prudent Annie had already paid for it.

I kept my promise to write to Annie. I sent her several letters, giving detailed accounts of my various activities, such as they were. I invited her to my wedding. I told her that Mary and I were expecting our first baby. I let her know that the daily help in London and the housekeeper who had replaced her in the country had none of her irreplaceable qualities. And I told her, correctly, that I missed her, and dared to say that if her brother died, she must surely come back to Mr Rudolf. I was to receive a single reply.

Glasgow, May 12

My dear Andrew,

You must be thinking what a very rude old Annie I am. You have written me such lovely letters and I haven't so much as picked up pen and paper to answer them. The truth is, my dear, that Bruce has been what we call a handful. He brings out the churchwoman in me, I am afraid to say, with his everlasting cursing. It is like looking after a bad-tempered child. Not that I have had much experience in that department, as they say, for you were never difficult, my poor lovely boy.

I have spoken to Mr Rudolf on the phone. He also gave me your good news. You tell me you miss me. Well, the feeling is mutual. I miss you both. Mr Rudolf was always a pleasure to work for until – My pen is running away with me – until he started having what I call his moods. He has changed. I tried more than once to tell him he has changed but he snapped at me and said he had things on his mind. Perhaps it was that wretched business with Charlie's son. Well, we all have things on our minds but we do our best to stay polite. Something has happened to him. But tell him I miss him. Will you please, Andrew?

Your beautiful English puts me to shame. No wonder Mr Rudolf is so proud of you. He has good reason to, what with the storms you have weathered.

Annie had used this phrase before. I had heard of the storms I had weathered when I was still her poor lovely, and little, boy. What storms had I weathered? I received my answer in 1948.

You must watch him closely whenever you can and try to keep him cheerful. He used to be Cheerfulness Itself but not any more. I worry for him. Try and care for him, will you Andrew, but not at a cost to yourself. You and Mary have your own lives to live. Well, there is a stream of words for you. I send you hugs and kisses, my poor lovely boy, which you will always be for me even though you are a grown man. I hear Bruce calling for me. He is a strain on the nerves and that is the truth.

Remember to tell Mr Rudolf I miss him as I miss you.

Yours, Annie.

Reading Annie's letter of fifty years ago, I see that she was alerting me, in her honest fashion, to the possibility of my becoming the very prisoner I was and am. I think she would have let her preposterously ailing brother rot in his self-created hell if Mr Rudolf hadn't changed character so inexplicably. She was content with Mr Rudolf the carefree rake, the fêted star of operetta, the dutiful uncle and the blasé man of the world to whom women posted their drawers.

It was the melancholic who confused and, perhaps, upset her. At nights, alone in her room, with Gavin's picture by her side, she too would have been prey to melancholy, to feelings of utter desolation. The happy-go-lucky Mr Rudolf had helped her expunge the worst of her memories – the vision of Gavin being blown to pieces on that day of barbarous slaughter. She had said as much to me over countless meals in the kitchen together.

— He's had me laughing with him since the moment he took me on. I often feel I'm acting in a funny play with him. He's kept me light-hearted, if anyone has, the scallywag.

After Annie's simple funeral service, I reminded my uncle that she had said her brother would never accept charity. The devil was in me, I suppose. Spurred on by my remark, he approached the bleary-eyed Bruce and said it was his intention, out of respect and for his love of Annie, to pay for everything. He was prepared to match the money she had already paid to the undertaker, with an added bonus to tide Bruce over. My uncle, in the saloon bar of the Young Pretender, wrote him a cheque for five hundred pounds.

Bruce accepted, tearfully, Mr Rudolf's charity.

o   o   o

— This is work for a dogsbody, said my uncle. You shouldn't be wasting your time with it.

— I'm not wasting my time. You couldn't be a recluse without me.

— If I stopped your salary, you would have to find a job more suited to your intelligence. I have a mind to throw you out of the house and let you fend for yourself.

This conversation took place every few months, with the words altered but the sentiments unchanged. It was usually light-hearted in tone. Yet once, I remember, he sounded genuinely angry – with himself as much as with me, it seemed.

— You're nearly thirty, my darling, and you've hardly begun to live. Tear yourself away from me, I beg of you. Go out and find another woman. Sow some more of your wild oats while you've got them to sow. I don't want to feel that I've hindered your progress.

— You haven't.

— How would you know? You haven't given your future without me a moment's thought.

It was true.

— Have you? he persisted.

— No.

— Then you should.

I saw no reason to, I said. I did not add that I still needed the protection his company gave me. I was not going to risk his getting angrier by stating the obvious. I could not imagine being with anyone else – however sympathetic, amusing or interesting.

— It worries me, Andrew, that you don't seem to want to be independent. I feel that I ought to be the mother bird and thrust you from the nest. I urge you to consider the future.

— I shall, I lied.

— Be sure you do.

The following morning he suggested we take a summer holiday together, to celebrate the depressing fact that we would each have a nought on our birthdays. He would be sixty in December, and I exactly half his age in January. My immediate future was therefore decided.

When my uncle broke the news I had been searching for in Andrei's dreams, my retreating parents stopped and turned towards me, their arms extended in anguished greeting. Their fate was mine, now.

— Mămică, Tată, I said to their shades.

My father's last letter to his brother is before me,

in its frayed and faded envelope. Although I know its contents, I lack the strength to pick it up. My hand reaches out for it, and then hesitates. The sight of his clerk's neat handwriting is more than I can presently bear, for even in distress he delighted in the look of the words he was using. I remember that Roman Petrescu was the town's *corespondent*, the calm and thoughtful man who took up his pen on behalf of the poor unlettered, of whom there were too many among us. They sat beside him at his desk in his tiny office in the *primărie*, marvelling at the exquisite shapes and forms he made out of what they were telling him to write to their distant relatives and loved ones. He remained a calligrapher to the day of his death, when he wrote only for himself. The elegance of his script still unnerves me. I would have preferred him to have gone wild in his grief, to have scratched at the sheet of hotel notepaper as he let his dearly beloved brother Rudi know of his impending plan to disappear. But he didn't, or couldn't. He had no truck with wildness. His despair was a stubborn thing.

I have pushed Tată's letter beneath a pile of photographs of Rudolf Peterson in his heyday. I am listening to the Golden Age compact disc as I examine them yet again, those mementoes of a time in my uncle's life when he was the toast of Vienna, Paris, Budapest and the capital of the country he would come to regard as beastly. He is casting roguish glances — I was the absolute master of the roguish glance, Andrew —

at Hilde Bernhard and the other leading ladies he charmed with his dark handsomeness and angelic voice. He is wearing all kinds of uniform – military, naval, regal, piratical (a fetching eye-patch) as well as the voluminous shirt and baggy trousers of the humane brigand. His face exhibits – I think that's the correct word – no sign of the melancholy that was already affecting him. He seems to be the happiest man in the world.

But that was before the events of February 1937, when Rudolf Peterson lost his brother and sister-in-law and gained possession of his nephew.

How old was I when Uncle Rudolf explained to me the difference between grand opera and the trivia in which, as he said, he had been enmeshed? I think I was sixteen. Not long before, he had given his hugely successful farewell performance, and his public had assumed he was now in retirement.

— Andrew, my darling, they don't know that I ache
to come back as Don José or Don Ottavio. Or Otello,
or Florestan, or Lohengrin. Or anybody other than
those fools in silly costumes I've impersonated for
twenty-five years. I want to sing music that expresses
more than idiotic patriotism or soppy romance. I want
to sing about real feelings, complicated emotions.
That's what I want to do before I die.

The plots of most operas are ludicrous, he went
on to say. Think of those convenient love potions;
those letters that arrive too late; those disguises that
anyone with an iota of intelligence would see through.
No matter. They are of no matter, those absurdities,
when set beside the many moments of truth they help
bring into being.

— There are no such moments in the stuff I've
wasted my time with. None at all. The sentiments
are trite and so is the music.

Then he talked, once again, of the days he spent in
the master's presence, with Koko the parrot awaiting
the opportunity to screech disapproval. He sang the
Flower Song for me, in the music room of his Sussex
house, just as – he remarked, with a grin – Jean de
Reszke had sung it for him between cigars. What
a charmed life Andrew Peters led, to have such a

tuneful protector, I often told myself. My school-
mates' fathers were doctors or lawyers or grocers or
journalists. None of them, I safely assumed, had the
voice of an angel. None of them serenaded their sons
the way my protector serenaded me.

I had seen the newspaper seller from Uncle Rudolf's
car, when Charlie was showing me the varied sights
of London. I could merely point at him, because I
lacked the new words to express my amazement at
his appearance. He looked much more interesting
than the statue of Eros Charlie was trying to tell
me about.

— They say he's the god of love.

But my eyes were fixed on the man without a nose,
standing in front of the London Pavilion, bawling out
News and Star, News and Star. I was mesmerised (a
new word I learned in school) by the sight of him.
The gap in his face held me spellbound. Each time
Charlie drove me through Piccadilly I stared and
stared, wanting an explanation for the newsvendor's
missing feature.

— He put something somewhere he shouldn't have,
Charlie said, and laughed. The phrase has stayed with
me thanks to the fact that Charlie repeated it so often.

— There he is, Andrew. He's the one who put something somewhere he shouldn't have.

Years later, after Charlie had gone from us, I mentioned the noseless man to Uncle Rudolf, and the mysterious observation Charlie used whenever we passed him.

— If ever anyone was an expert at putting something somewhere he shouldn't have, it was Charlie. That unfortunate newspaper seller – who, I seem to remember, was pretty cheerful, given his circumstances – had caught syphilis in the days before the discovery of penicillin. The disease must have been untreated to have done such damage to him. It killed Schubert, my darling.

I learned, that winter afternoon, about the dangers of uninhibited sex, of which busy little Eros, his bow at the permanent ready, was the pagan god. It had struck my uncle as a cruel irony that the poor wretch's pitch was in Piccadilly, so near to a statue that was intended to represent the Angel of Christian Charity, though ordinary folk knew, or imagined, otherwise.

— You won't lose your nose, Andrew. Believe me. You may well lose your heart, but that's an altogether nicer matter.

I did not lose my heart to Mary, as everyone

assumed, for the brief period of our lonely marriage. I was thirty, and divorced, when I arrived at the realization that it was irretrievably lost. In a hotel in Sapri, on the Tyrrhenian coast, I understood, with terrified delight, that the man who slept beside me was my only love. There could not, and would never be, another.

The previous day, we had sat outside a trattoria in Salerno, admiring the blue-eyed transvestites parading past. The clickety-clack of their high heels on the cobbles sounded, Uncle Rudolf observed, like some improbable piece for solo xylophone. Despite the intense heat, many of the tall, broad-shouldered make-believe society ladies were draped in furs.

And then, on that abiding Saturday, we drove across the rough, barren countryside, stopping once to eat grilled swordfish and drink chilled red wine at a roadside shack. We reached Sapri at dusk and decided to pass the night in the tiny seaside town. To our astonishment, all the hotels were full, with the exception of one – the Vittoria – that offered us an attic with a double bed. It seemed there was a wedding in progress, and later that evening, as we strolled around the bay, we were invited to join in the celebrations. A table was set out and laid for us on the promenade, and soon we were the most cheerful of guests. A band was playing, and we noticed that many of the girls were dancing with each other, and that a few brave, but embarrassed, boys were doing the same.

— They are very strict Catholics here, Andrew. They aren't married, you see. Oh, such sweet innocence.

My uncle danced with a plump, tightly-corseted widow who sat with us afterwards. She spoke no English and her Italian, Uncle Rudolf explained, was of the sawn-off Southern kind, with everyday words invariably sliced in half. He had mastered the language in Vienna, he told her, at the start of his singing career.

— You are a singer?

— I was.

She rose from the chair with the word *Aspett'*. *Aspett'* she shrieked again and again as she ran between the dancers, one of whom she caused to fall over. She did not turn to apologize but continued running, her cries of *Aspett'* increasing in volume. We did as she ordered, and waited. When she returned, breathless, it was in the company of the bride and bridegroom and their parents. They rushed to embrace Uncle Rudolf, to pat his back, to shake his hands. They implored him to sing. He replied that his voice was a shadow of its former self, and the bridegroom responded by saying that the gentleman's shadow would be very welcome. My uncle, draining his glass, nodded assent.

I watched, entranced, as they dragged him over the dance floor to the smiling band. He had no means of escape. Somebody's father – the bride's or groom's, I forget which – took hold of a microphone and asked for silence. The famous Signor Rudolfo from Vienna was going to sing for them. It was their great fortune he was visiting Sapri that evening. Sapri was not a place great singers came to, but here he was, in the flesh, and would they greet him?

The microphone was switched off, at my uncle's request. He sang a few notes of *Funiculi, funiculà* before the pianist began to accompany him. He basked in the generous applause that followed. Then, elated, he broke into – literally, broke into – *E lucevan le stelle* from Puccini's *Tosca*. He had never played Cavaradossi on stage, but here – in this remote seaport in Southern Italy – he was singing of stars brightly shining, as indeed they were at that very moment. He gave, unaccompanied, the most beautiful rendering of *Dalla sua pace* I'd ever heard in all the years he had been singing it for me, and then came the Romanian song about the Carpathian shepherd sighing for love of the dead girl in the snow. When he reached the end, the wedding guests were too moved to applaud immediately. Uncle Rudolf bowed and bowed and blew kisses to his unexpected audience and with a cry of *Basta, grazie* he stepped down from the dais.

He was weeping with joy while his ebullient admirers surrounded him. The bride, Giuliana, and the groom, Piero, thanked him fulsomely, and soon he was sitting between them at the head table, the absolute guest of honour. He had sung, in Sapri, the music he felt he should have sung in Paris, London and New York, and now he was being fêted by people who would not have heard his voice – his angel's voice – in any of the great opera houses. He had achieved an absurd, but genuine, recognition. I saw that he glowed. He beckoned me to him with a flamboyant, drunken gesture, and introduced me, his handsome and clever nephew, to the new husband and wife. I listened as he talked of his time in Nice, understanding most of what he said, having heard it so often in English. He spoke without a trace of his usual sadness, making everyone near him laugh with his impersonation of Koko's critical screech. The parents knew nothing of Jean de Reszke – Caruso, yes; Gigli, yes – so Uncle Rudolf described him, emphasizing the master's delight in the word 'belly', and his habit of singing snatches from his greatest roles between cigars. *La fleur que tu m'avais jetée* sang my uncle, the Don José who never was, rising from his chair and swaying slightly. There was more applause, more backslapping, and yet more wine for Signor Rudolfo of Vienna to drink.

Who will ever read what I write next? Only my son, perhaps, before he burns or throws away these pages. In the early hours of that Sunday morning in the summer of 1960, I steered my uncle in the direction of the hotel. Our progress up the stairs leading to the attic was long and arduous, since he was now almost incapable of movement. I remember that I pulled him up the very last flight and dragged him into the room. I lifted him up from the floor and somehow got him on to the bed, where I undressed him. He was laughing an idiot's laugh as I removed his shoes, socks and trousers.

— Allow me to take off my shirt, he mumbled and instantly fell asleep.

He was naked eventually, except for his underpants. Why did I lower him out of them? I suppose I was recalling those warm nights in my childhood when he held the shivering, frightened Andrei in his arms. He had worn nothing then. I was safe from the cruel world of blinding light, wrapped up as I was in his hairiness. I lay down beside him in the Vittoria, and realized that I had not slept alongside him for fifteen years.

He awoke for a second, muttering:

— *Buona notte, carissimo.*

He attempted to kiss me, I think, but then sleep overtook him.

I lay there, no longer the bewildered Andrei whose Mamă and Tată would not turn to look at him. I was a man of thirty, not the little boy so desperately in need of protection. My protector was beside me, snoring loudly. And as I lay there, near to him, I thought of all those countless times I had touched him, expressing silent thanks for the care he had taken of me. I stroked his arm, softly, and realized with something close to terror that I was aching with desire for him. I wanted my uncle to do to me what he had done to Hilde Bernhard and the other women in his life. I wanted him to possess me. I wanted to be his.

I lay there, as still as if I were dead, with the knowledge that I was irreparably in love with Uncle Rudolf and that such a love could not be physically gratified. Not ever. It was doomed to be unrequited. Even so, I moved nearer to him, until our legs were meeting. I lifted the sheet from us, because the room was hot and we were both sweaty. I looked at that part of his body I had only looked at innocently before and saw that it was hard. Was he dreaming of one of his many conquests? I dared to brush it with my fingertips. When it stirred, I withdrew my hand, terrified by what I had done, or might go on doing. I remembered, as I stared at it, that he had once said I had my mother's beauty, and the ache inside me returned with unbearable force. I lay there beside him, powerless. Then, as I went on staring, listening to his repertoire of drunken snores, I slowly and steadily eased myself. It was all I could do, I reasoned. Anything else was unthinkable.

I left the bed and went to the wash basin, where I gazed on his smiling face with the eyes of a hopeless lover.

I dressed and went out to watch the dawn rising over the bay. I felt radiant and abject by turns. In the first light of a new day, I was aware that I had a secret to keep from my truthful companion.

— Be kind to your uncle, Andrew darling. His head is spinning and his stomach is sending him the kind of alarming messages that are frowned on in polite company. You will have to drive us on to Naples.

— My pleasure, I said. That will be my pleasure.

— Tell me about the pirate.

— Which pirate would that be?

He knew exactly which pirate I meant.

— The one in the photograph Tată gave the guard.

— Oh, *him*. *That* pirate. His name, if I have to remember it yet again, you scamp, was Shahar. He was the hero of *The Balkan Buccaneer*.

In the original libretto, my uncle said, the Balkan country of which the swashbuckling Shahar was heir to the throne was called Tragscabia.

— Let's have a history lesson, Andrew. The 'T' is for Turkey, the 'r' for Romania, the 'a' Albania, the 'g' for Greece, the 's' for Serbia, the 'c' Croatia and the 'b' for Bulgaria. We disposed of Tragscabia at the first rehearsal. Everyone agreed it sounded like a nasty

skin disease. After much head-banging, we came up
with Balkania as Shahar's homeland.

— How did he know he was the heir to the throne,
Uncle Rudolf?

— He didn't.

— When did he find out?

— You know the answer. I've told you a dozen
times at least.

— Tell me again, please.

— There was a sea battle on stage after the second interval, during the course of which I, Shahar,
rescued the kidnapped Princess Melina from the
clutches of my rival pirate, the wicked Dimitrios,
and his evil-looking crew. His ship, *The Firebrand*,
and mine, *The Vengeance*, collided mid-stage. There
was a lot of smoke to disguise the fact that the singer
playing Dimitrios was useless at fencing. He had to
strike a blow which ripped open my shirt to expose
the purple birthmark on my right shoulder. I usually
did the ripping myself when the smoke was at its
thickest.

— What happened then?

— Well, the Princess Melina, now safely aboard
The Vengeance, saw the birthmark and cried out 'My
king! My long-lost king!' before fainting away from

the shock. I, Shahar, brought her back to life with
a passionate kiss – which the audience applauded
at every performance – and shouted 'My gleaming
cutlass has won the day and the love of Princess
Melina!' to the cheers of my fellow pirates. Is that
enough for you, you scamp?

— Yes and no, Uncle Rudolf. I want to hear the
silly song.

— Do you? Then you're a glutton for punishment.
Just this once. *The Balkan Buccaneer* ended, God
help me, with your wretched uncle strutting down to
the footlights with his bride-to-be and singing – wait
for it, Andrew – and singing:

> *I was a pirate, but now I'm a king,*
> *My ship has come to port –*
> *It's of freedom and peace and love I sing*
> *As I go to greet my court*
>
> *Melina will be my dearest wife*
> *And I her carefree spouse –*
> *The Balkanian throne will be ours for life*
> *In that happiest royal house.*
>
> *Hurrah for Melina, hurrah for me,*
> *The one-time King of the Sea!*

Now go to sleep, Andrew.

— Where was the water, Uncle Rudolf?

— Which water?

— The ocean. The sea. How did you get the sea on the stage?

— We didn't. We had rippling waves on a blue backdrop. That was our Mediterranean. I'll leave the door ajar, he promised, before kissing me goodnight.

I loved to hear the story of Shahar, the pirate who came to be king of Balkania. My uncle first told it to me when I was eight or nine and repeated it often, at my request, in the years leading up to my adolescence, when he decided that I was too old and too intelligent for it and he too weary to be bothered with the silly song. But that was not the end of *The Balkan Buccaneer*. On my uncle's seventy-third birthday, he and I and Bogdan Rangu went to a performance of Bach's Christmas Oratorio, and afterwards had dinner at a French restaurant in Soho. Uncle Rudolf had been gloomy all day, talking of wasted time and lost opportunities, but the music, the food, the wine and the cheerful company of Bogdan caused him to be happy in an especially lively way. He insisted on Bogdan returning to the house by the Thames for a nightcap. Very late in the evening, over his third or fourth Armagnac, Bogdan announced that of all the nonsensical pieces his dear friend had appeared in *The Balkan Buccaneer* was his particular favourite.

— Oh, I still chortle when I think of Rudi fighting that duel on the creaking ship. Oh, and that vivid – or do I mean livid? – birthmark.

— Both, Bogdan. It was both.

— And those crinkly waves. And those other pirates, with curtain rings in their ears. Your crew had shiny white teeth, I remember, Rudi, but the crew of your enemy —

— Dimitrios —

— Yes, Dimitrios. He was so fat. His crew had teeth that were black or gold or missing.

— That was to show they were villains.

— Naturally. Evidently. You should have seen it, Andrew. You should have been born a bit earlier so that you could have seen it.

— Uncle told me the story many times, Bogdan. I even know the words to the song he sang at the finale.

— You do? asked Bogdan.

— I bet you don't.

— Shall we sing it together, Uncle?

— Oh, please, please, Bogdan entreated.

— I'm drunk enough to say yes.

We sang Shahar's rousing farewell song to my uncle's unsteady piano accompaniment. I have to say that I had a better command of the lyrics, because he faltered on the line about the Balkanian throne. When we had finished, Bogdan clapped loudly and demanded an encore – which we provided, word-perfect.

— You were wonderful, Andrew.

— And me, Bogdan?

— Hilarious, Rudi. As ever.

— You rogue.

— What a treat for an ancient surrealist. What an absurd and delightful treat.

Bogdan did not attend my uncle's funeral two and a half years later. He sent me his fondest commiserations and promised faithfully that he would be available for his own cremation.

Of all my uncle's friends, it was Bogdan I saw most of after his death. We always spoke in French.

— I tried to explain to Rudi that where operetta was concerned the Jews had the last laugh.

— What do you mean?

— Rudi was unhappy to sing that nationalistic

trivia because it reminded him of the horrors it pre-saged. The irony is that the majority of the composers and librettists of operetta were Jewish. They were having fun at the expense of the very people who hated them. And 'expense' is the appropriate word. They made a huge amount of money, because oper-etta – however bad, like *The Balkan Buccaneer* of blessed memory – was immensely popular. This information, alas, did not ease the pain of your uncle's old age.

Bogdan's death, in his ninetieth year, received greater coverage in the newspapers than had Uncle Rudolf's in 1975. He was hailed as one of the supreme surrealists – more serious, and seriously inventive, than Salvador Dali, and in some ways the equal of René Magritte. His funeral, at a London crema-torium, was characteristically anarchic and inspired. The distinguished mourners – artists, writers, exiled poets and philosophers – were pleased to see what looked like television cameras recording the sad event as they entered the Chapel of Rest and took their places for the service. But there was no service, although an obviously drunken clergyman, his left elbow perched on the coffin, sat silent – apart from the odd belch – throughout. Bogdan had issued

instructions that a film be shot of his final departure. It would be, he hoped, the crowning artistic
achievement of his ridiculously long life.

As soon as the congregation was seated, the doors
were shut and the non- or anti-service began. The
spluttering laughter of a baby was heard, and this
was followed by a boy and girl sharing an hysterical
exchange – he saying 'Don't be silly'; she 'Don't make
me laugh' – which continued until they were both
beyond words. The guffaws of some men in a bar or
pub came next, above the much-repeated punchline
of a dirty joke: 'The genie thought I was asking for a
twelve-inch pianist.'

Bogdan's dying wish, it transpired, was that the
friends, acquaintances and admirers gathered at
Mortlake would be so infected by the taped laughter
coming at them from every direction that they, too,
would be convulsed. They were. The tape finished
with a forceful raspberry executed by Bogdan himself, and then the clergyman drained the whisky
bottle in his right hand and seemed to pass out. The
coffin disappeared to the strains of 'Ta-ra-ra-boom-
de-ay', and everybody rose and cheered.

I hosted the wake in the house that was now mine.
We drank surrealist cocktails, created by Bogdan,

which the caterers were almost afraid to serve us. The clergyman appeared, completely sober, revealing that he was an actor and that the whisky he had consumed during the bizarre proceedings was cold tea. He now intended to get seriously plastered, and achieved his ambition with surprising speed, thanks to Bogdan's Franco-Russian Fantasy, a mixture of claret, sparkling Saumur and vodka. I was approached at the buffet table by a young man who introduced himself as Mischa Smith, the founder and manager of Golden Age Records. It was an honour, he said, to be among so many souvenirs of the legendary Rudolf Peterson, whose voice he had first heard as a small boy. He was still entranced by it. He asked me, tremulously, if I was my uncle's executor.

— I am.

— Would you give me permission to bring out a CD made up of his Vienna recordings?

— I can't. He never recorded the music he really loved. He wanted his voice forgotten.

— It mustn't be, Mr Peters. That would be criminal.

After seven months of persuasive phone calls, as well as lunches and visits to the opera, I relented.

— He *has* to be preserved for posterity. You know
he has.

— Hand me the contract while I'm not having
second thoughts.

I signed. We toasted the signing with Uncle Rudolf's
champagne.

— Forgive me, I mumbled, out of Mischa's hearing. I was apologizing for my treachery.

Rudolf Peterson is famous again. No, that's wrong.
He is now celebrated by the discerning people who
idolize Jussi Björling, Heddle Nash and Axel Schültz.
He has joined the pantheon of lyric tenors. I have
brought him home, against his wishes.

I came to love my uncle when he was leonine
in appearance, his abundant white hair in need of
frequent cutting. I had loved him before, of course, in
his paternal role as my protector. My protector from
what? I had known, in some deep place inside me,
that when I arrived in London in 1937, my life and
world had altered drastically. Were the revelations
eleven years afterwards – of my mother's murder; my
father's willed drowning – cruelly delayed? It would
seem so, from what I have written of the dreams that
plagued me. I heard, later, that Annie had urged him
to break the terrible news years earlier – when I was

ten, for instance. But my uncle found it impossible
to comply. He would wait, he said, until I was a
confident English youth. Roman and Irina Petrescu
would have to remain lost or missing.

My son Billy regards his great-uncle's long silence
as unforgivable, despite my protestations to the con-
trary. When he poured me that second medicinal
brandy, Uncle Rudolf's face showed all the pain and
guilt that being secretive had caused him. I think
he knew he had protected me too well. Perhaps,
on one of those nights when Andrei was deserted
on that snowy plain and woke up as Andrew in
a chilly sweat, he should have carried me to his
bed, laid me down, and told me the truth. Perhaps he often intended to, but the prospect of my
young heart being broken beyond repair may have
stopped him saying the words that were there to
be said.

It was Billy who suggested, in December 1989,
that I ought to go back to Romania, now that the
revolution had ended a reign of tyranny. I had no
need, then, to see the town where I was born and
to stand in the market place in which the red-faced
woman had taunted my mother. He made the suggestion again when he telephoned to wish me well

on my seventieth birthday in January, and this time I replied that I would consider it.

My flight is booked. I shall be leaving on the ninth of September. If I don't tear up the tickets, that is.

Uncle Rudolf's last word was my mother's name.

— Irina, he whispered.

His eyes were looking into mine, but it was the girl who gained his brother's love he was seeing.

— Irina Aderca, my darling. Irina, he gasped.

I kept my hand in his for long minutes after his death. Then I stood up and kissed his forehead.

— Goodbye.

How inadequate and how nonsensical it sounded, that choked 'goodbye'. He had craved the enduring release of death, and now that urgent wish had been granted. I was saying goodbye to his tired body, but to nothing else. I knew, even as I spoke, that I would remain imprisoned until the time of my own release, whenever that was due. Twenty-five years on, I am still awaiting it.

The Irina he spoke to at the end had yet to become my mother. She was the pretty Domnişoara Aderca, the daughter of Josef, who was known to the older people in the town as the Debt Collector. My presence was obliterated as he gazed lovingly at her, the sweetly innocent girl who would one day prefer to live with a clerk in a humdrum backwater rather than share the fame and fortune of a singer who had apartments in Vienna, Paris and London. From his hospital bed, he saw her restored to her adolescent self, and I was pleased that his final glimpse of the irreplaceable Irina was not of the pregnant woman left to die in the forest. Or so I understood by his saying Aderca, not Petrescu.

In November 1975, I followed my uncle's instructions and took his ashes to Nice, where I scattered them, handful by handful, beneath the palm trees along the Promenade des Anglais – those same palm trees he had counted that other November morning, as with fear in his heart and a piece of bloodied paper on his chin, he made his way towards his destiny. He had relished the idea of his remains joining the hot dust, and I sent them from me with the vision of his youthful fervour in mind, the fervour of someone whose ambition it was to be the finest lyric tenor in the world. I tossed the urn that had recently contained the corporeal Rudi Petrescu or Rudolf Peterson into the glittering sea and watched it bobbing there until a motorboat spawned large waves that consigned it to the depths. My duty was done.

I live here with everything that was, and is, Uncle Rudolf's, in the house that is now his shrine. It's a shrine he himself created, and which I could not dismantle, as he advised me to, once he was dead.

— Sell the paintings and drawings, Andrew, but look after Bogdan's collage for me. I can't bear to think of a stranger owning it.

Years earlier, he had attempted to destroy the photographs that charted his career in operetta. I had rescued them with the simplest of arguments.

— You can tear them up, Uncle, but you can't wipe out your memories, however hard you try. I'll lock them away in a drawer upstairs, so you don't have to see them.

— As you wish.

— I shall need them if I decide to write your biography.

— Let me rest, Andrew. Even in death, let me rest, he said histrionically. I sound very Shakespearean, don't I?

Nothing has been sold; nothing destroyed. How Billy will dispose of his inheritance, I can only guess.

For now, the shrine – with its solitary living occupant – is still intact.

— Come and sit down, Andrew. I have things to tell you. I am going to pour you a large brandy. You may not like the taste at first, but I am sure it will calm your nerves.

— I'm calm enough, Uncle. Why shouldn't I be? I'm not in the least nervous.

— Come and sit down, my darling. As I say, I have things to tell you, if I can.

I was confused, and said so. He advised me to sip my drink.

— It is time you were told the truth, Andrew – the truth I have been protecting you from since that evening in February 1937 when I took you up in my arms on Victoria Station. You will have to be patient with me. This is as painful an experience for me as it will be for you. But the time for telling the truth has come, and I mustn't delay it any longer.

It was necessary to begin with a history lesson, he explained. It would be a grim history lesson, but it might also help to put the truth he had to tell me in some kind of perspective.

— Perspective, my darling, he sneered. Some kind of terrible perspective.

He reminded me that my maternal grandfather, Josef Aderca, the one they called the Debt Collector, was Jewish.

— In the beastly country of our birth, Andrew, the Jews were blamed for every wrong. There was scarcely a single political crime they hadn't committed. They spread diseases, and they stole money from the poor. I heard these opinions or sentiments wherever I went. I heard them at their shrillest in Vienna, on the lips of rich ladies gorging cream cakes and strudel. You couldn't escape the filth. There were pogroms in our beastly country, and in Poland, and in Hungary. In Russia, too. The victims were almost always Jews, my darling.

He was silent. I waited to learn what the truth had to do with pogroms.

— Irina, your mother, Andrew, your beautiful mother, was murdered, my dear.

— Murdered? Who by?

— By three men who were seen dragging her into the forest outside the town. It was a pogrom in miniature, I suppose. They stripped her naked and raped her. One of them slit her throat. She was left to die in the snow. A boy with a dog discovered her body.

— And Tată? I asked. And Tată?

— Roman sent me a telegram with the news. *Some* of the news. I agreed to look after you, to give you a lovely holiday while he tried to come to terms with his grief. It was a grief I shared, but I hid it from you. I had to. Roman never came to terms with it. Have you the strength, my darling, to read the last letter he wrote to me?

I nodded.

— It's in the language we don't speak any more. If you have trouble with the words, I will translate them for you.

I had no trouble with the words themselves, only with their meaning.

Beloved Rudi. I am in Paris still. I do not intend to return to Botoşani. I do not intend to return to Romania. I do not intend to leave Paris. I am giving myself to the Seine.
Irina was bearing our second child. Think of it Rudi. Think of what they did to her. I think of nothing else.
On the train to Bucharest we met an Iron

Guardist in his green shirt. There was massacre in his eyes. That is what I saw.

Andrei will have a life worth living with you, my dearest brother. Perhaps you will teach him to sing.

Please come to Paris to identify me. I am leaving a note at the hotel reception desk to be forwarded to the police. I will have drowned by the time you receive this. You and Andrei have all the love that is left in me. Say the word IGLOOS to him. Your Roman.

I looked up and shivered. Then, through tears, I saw Mamă and Tată in that blinding whiteness. They stopped and turned to gaze at their son, whom they greeted with outstretched arms. I fell into those arms, which seemed to reclaim me as I sat there on that August evening.

— Mămică, Tată, I said to their shades.

I was theirs again, and the whiteness was gone.

— I want to eat cabbage soup, Uncle Rudolf.

— I'll get Annie to make you some. It won't taste like Irina's.

— No. That doesn't matter. You didn't say 'igloos' to me.

— That's true. Shall I say it now? 'Igloos', my darling.

I told him, then, about the pictures of igloos in Tată's magazine, and how the peasants' huts, covered in snow, made me think of them on that train journey when we met the man with massacre in his eyes.

I drank another brandy, which my uncle described as medicinal, and later on we ate the soup our resourceful Annie had prepared with a cabbage from the garden.

— All it lacks is soured cream, my uncle confided. I have another treat in store for you as soon as you've cleaned your bowl.

He led me to the music room, opened the piano, and sang *Waft her, angels*. It was Irina Petrescu and her unborn child, not Jephtha's daughter, who were being sacrificed, though neither of us remarked on it.

In my dreams that night the icon stayed on the wall and Andrei had no cause to pursue his parents, who remained close beside him. But the woman in the market let out her usual taunts – as she did this morning, when I summoned up the courage to recall what my uncle chose to tell me on the tenth of August 1948.

❖   ❖   ❖

I came to understand, in the years of Uncle Rudolf's continuing musical re-education, the nature of the profound distaste he felt for the culture in which operetta had flourished. He had been party to a despicable frivolousness, he said. The gypsies he'd impersonated weren't real, because they all turned out to be kings or princes or barons, and what were the brigands he'd played but a bunch of rabid nationalists, crude beasts for ever casting roguish glances at love-sick, lunatic maidens? In the streets of Vienna, Bucharest and Budapest, a black operetta was being enacted daily while he was behind the footlights singing of a liberty and freedom indistinguishable from tyranny. He had betrayed not only Jean de Reszke and Georges Enesco, but his own best instincts as well. He had sung the kind of music that was enjoyed by those who brought about Europe's destruction. Such was his conviction in old age, which I refrained from arguing against.

There was a different kind of music to savour. We were a familiar sight, the two of us, in the capital's recital rooms, concert halls and opera houses. Uncle Rudolf craved a 'melodious dissonance', as he termed it, now. It was there in Alban Berg and Janáček and his adored Bartók, and it cheered his otherwise depressed spirits. He relished the serious playfulness of Martinu and Ligeti, two survivors of a pogrom-ridden past. He listened with a rapt attentiveness that beatified his features. He was as much a student as I was during those hours in which his melancholy was shaken off or cast aside or not even contemplated.

In the silent hours, though, his mind turned to what he deemed his one great failure in life – his inability to persuade my stubborn father to leave a country overcome by demons.

— Roman was an absurd optimist. He said I was a false prophet when I warned him of the troubles ahead. I'd seen the signs and heeded the hateful words in Vienna and knew which way the Fascist wind was blowing. I think he altered his opinion when he heard Codreanu ranting in the town square, but by then it was almost too late. Almost, but not quite. I put out one last hand to him a month or so before – before the forest and then the bridge – but he resisted it. I should have gone there and forced them out. That's what I should have done, Andrew.

On the evening my uncle rechristened me Andrew, he was ignorant of Tată's plan to give himself to the Seine. The letter containing this desolate information reached Nightingale Mansions after his death. Yet Uncle Rudolf had had an inkling that my holiday in England would be permanent, such was the weariness in my father's voice when they discussed my immediate future on the telephone. This inkling would soon be an undoubted fact. By calling me Andrew on the twenty-third of February, 1937, he was severing me in some measure from the beastly country of my birth. What's in a name? A new identity, perhaps. He was determined that I should benefit from an English education, and that the rest of my boyhood should be carefree and fruitful. Which – Andrei's blindingly white dreams apart – it was.

— I have a pain in my stomach, Andrei, my uncle said, in the old words, on the morning of the sixteenth of March, 1975. He was doubled up on his bedroom floor, clutching his gut. Andrei, he repeated, fetch a doctor or get me to the hospital. And again in the old words.

That was the end of his calling me Andrew, and the start of his final illness. Morphine was to be his comforter, not the soothing dissonance that captured the dark soul of a blighted Europe. Whenever he regained consciousness, he spoke the language he had renounced before his nephew's arrival. And then, at the very last, it was my mother's eyelashes he recognized in wonderment, not mine.

There is a Hotel Minerva in the town where I was born, and I am staying in room 32 until tomorrow. I spent yesterday in Botoșani, the nearby city in which my parents shopped for clothes and furniture. I sat for a while in the park, and remembered that my mother, on that far-off summer afternoon, had said no to my father's suggestion that we hire a boat and take it out on the lake. Had Roman forgotten that she was terrified of water?

— It's not the sea, Irina, he had assured her. Look at that handsome lifeguard. I am confident that he would be delighted to rescue you.

Mama laughed, and remarked that if she ever needed rescuing she would rely on her own handsome husband to do it.

My mother had brought a bowl of *murături* – yes, that is the old word – and spread out a rug on the grass for us to sit on. We ate the delicately pickled vegetables on little plates, I recall, and drank sharp-tasting lemonade. My father was allowed to have his weekly glass of beer, and Mamă and I wondered how long it would be before he fell asleep.

— We shall tickle you if you do, Roman. Be warned.

— Oh no, not that. Spare me from that. My father put on the silly, frightened expression I loved.

As he pretended to doze, providing the occasional snore to add to the effect, we went to work on his ankles and his chin, an especially sensitive spot. Our tickling session soon followed its usual pattern, however, with Tată waking up as if from a nightmare, saying:

— I will have my revenge, you scamp.

His revenge, happily anticipated by me, was to lift my shirt and run his fingers across my bare tummy until I was weak with giggling.

As I sat there, in the same park where that scene, once submerged in memory, had taken place, I was stirred out of reverie by sounds of shouting and cheering. I reasoned they were coming from the city's main square, some streets away. I knew that a presidential election was in progress – it was the all-pervading subject in the newspapers I had attempted to read – and so I decided to join the crowd and listen to the speeches that were finding such deafening favour. I hurried along Strada Eminescu, named after the national poet who was born in the nearby town of Ipoteşti in 1850, and mingled with the now-silent men, women and children who were concentrating on the words a fat man dressed entirely in white was declaiming.

During my stay in the country of my birth, I have not been completely at ease with the old words. So many are unknown to me, and others that I knew in childhood have had to be dredged up with difficulty from the recesses of my clouded mind. Yet certain words have never gone, as I quickly realized as I listened to the gross politician in his angel's outfit. He was echoing, this more physically substantial Pied Piper, what Codreanu had said sixty-four years earlier in this very region, to the intense dismay of Irina and Roman Petrescu, among – I hope – others. I heard *evreu* and *evreiesc* and *cămătar* (meaning usurer), and then *ţigan*. My ears were alert to the filth my uncle had referred to so often, and they absorbed every nuance of the hate-filled rhetoric. The purity of Romania, as exemplified by the white shirt, the white suit, the white shoes, had to be restored, and that restoration could only happen as soon as every foreigner – every Jew and gypsy and drug-dealing Turk – had been expelled from her borders. Romanian purity had for too long been sullied by Western decadence and Russian domination and American materialism, but for not much longer.

I stared about me in that admiring crowd and my eyes settled on a plump, pink-faced woman who reminded me of the one who has plagued my dreams for most of my life. Was this her daughter, perhaps? The woman's eyes met mine, and suddenly she was at my side, kissing me on the cheek.

— He is a beast, she murmured. — And they are beasts also who cheer him. May he burn in hell.

To my shame, I suspected that she was leading me into a trap, in which I would be exposed as one of those foreigners the diabolical angel was haranguing.

— He belongs to our dark history, she said. — He should never have come out of it.

— Yes, I managed. — Yes, you are right. I agree with you.

Once the crowd was dispersed, and the fat vision of whiteness manoeuvred into a limousine that smacked of Western decadence and materialism, I invited Denisa to drink with me in a *cafenea*. I insisted on paying for the coarse red wine, as an unspoken apology for assuming she might be a reincarnation of the harridan who had upset my mother at the time the slimmer Pied Piper was extolling that impossible, implausible Romanian purity.

She is a teacher of English, so we chatted, in a mixture of our two languages, about her political disillusionment and the twin tragedy that ensured my freedom. The case of Irina Petrescu was familiar to her, though of my father's suicide and my uncle's fame she knew nothing.

I learned, only yesterday, that the three men who dragged Mamă into the forest never stood trial. They served in the army, and returned to the town as respectable Communist citizens, according to Denisa, who has taught their grandchildren. She went on to say that my mother's death is referred to in a footnote in a controversial book about the origins of Nazism. Her name, and her fate, had not been forgotten.

After my friendly parting with Denisa, I walked in the direction of the railway station. I passed houses Eminescu might have visited in his youth, and stopped in front of a boarded-up synagogue. Had the Adercas worshipped inside? It was likely, I answered myself, because they were part of a large

Jewish community, born and raised in Botoşani. The future Debt Collector would have come here to pray before he lost the faith of his fathers and put his trust in reason and doubt.

I am writing in another, grander hotel in Bucharest. My pilgrimage – for such, I think, it was – is almost over. The market place in the town evoked no horrors, for I had had a surfeit of those in my dreams. I saw only cobblestones, and they failed to upset me. I tried to picture the woman with the everlasting taunts, but – thanks to Denisa, perhaps – she remained unseen and unheard. A stroll in the forest proved no more productive of anguish. I was, I have to say, alarmingly placid: beyond tears and, for the present, above bitterness. I had wept on the Pont Marie during the trip that culminated with the recital by Dinu Lipatti, my protective uncle's most thoughtful of all thoughtful gifts to his displaced nephew. The man who had wasted Rudi Petrescu's God-given talent had borne me into the presence of one who, even on the brink of extinction, had gloriously honoured his. I caught myself humming the Bach partita he had played that September day, and felt a curious peace instead of the deep unrest I had expected.

— Mămică, Tată, I said, and added 'Nene'.

And then, humming once more, accompanied by my own dear trio, I put the trees behind me and returned to the Hotel Minerva under a cloudless sky.

What led me, this morning, into a shop on the Street of Victories? The icons displayed in the dusty window, those remnants of an Orthodoxy my mother espoused so fervently, were invitation enough. The door, which was locked with a security device, opened magically when I removed my hand from it. I entered, and was surrounded by a hundred or more likenesses of Christ, of the Virgin, of St Peter, St Nicholas, and other bearded divines I could not identify.

With the wizened shopkeeper's permission, I took down from the wall an icon of the Virgin and Child. The initials AI – Aderca Irina – had been etched by her unbelieving Jewish father into the wood on the back. They were faintly visible.

— You have dollars or Deutschmarks? asked the man, acknowledging my excitement.

— It's an inferior work, was my response.

— You did not examine it. You were more interested in what you saw behind it.

— How much do you want?

— How are you paying?

— In sterling.

— A thousand.

— A thousand?

— A thousand.

I offered him my credit card.

— Cash.

— Cash?

— Of course. I have no faith in plastic.

Three hours later, when I had paid the man whose faith resides in tangible money, and after he had wrapped my mother's icon in rough brown paper, I enquired, casually:

— How did you acquire this?

— The Securitate. A secret policeman. He brought a sackful of the things from Moldavia. It's quite a place for icons. Shall I put you on my mailing list?

— I think not, I answered, waking with empty hands.

I am finished with writing. The words that once raced across these pages have stopped in their contented tracks. I have attained some kind of rest because of them. I no longer fear waking to blood and snow and storks on chimney tops. I eat my burnt toast at breakfast, as I have eaten it since the morning of the twenty-fourth of February 1937, with a renewed sense of Uncle Rudolf's protective love for me. And mine, for him.

Let the bleak dreams come again, if they must, for I can cope with them now, unless I go gaga, as lonely people in their seventies do.

But I'm not lonely, as I have discovered. I have the warmth of the dead in which to bask.